MO, LOTTIE
and the Junkers

MO, LOTTIE
and the Junkers

by Jennifer Killick

Firefly

First published in 2019
by Firefly Press
25 Gabalfa Road, Llandaff North, Cardiff, CF14 2JJ
www.fireflypress.co.uk

A CIP catalogue record of this book is available from
the British Library.

print ISBN: 978-1-910080-92-4
ebook ISBN: 978-1-910080-93-1

This book has been published with the support of the
Welsh Books Council.

Typeset by: Elaine Sharples
Original cover art by Gareth Conway
Cover design by Kathryn Davies

Printed in Bulgaria by Pulsio Print

For my nephew, Alfie.

Opening the Box

This box belongs to Mo and Lottie
DO NOT OPEN,
EXCEPT IN AN EMERGENCY
(for example: if we have been imprisoned,
abducted or violently murdered.)

INSTRUCTIONS

1 Open box
2 Locate USB stick and insert into relevant computer port (a.k.a. the memory-stick hole)
3 Open folder named 'Junkers' (password is JUNKERSSUCK!!! – all caps, no spaces. [Lottie's idea])
4 Locate the AV clip 'Mo and Lottie: Our Vlog'. Press play – further instructions will follow.
5 Do not look at anything else in the box until we say!
6 Really, though, don't, or it won't make sense.
7 Everything else is in your hands.
P.S. – thanks and good luck 😊

x x x from Lottie and Mo x x x

File accessed…

Restricted folder…

Password required…

Enter password:

****

Password accepted…

Select file…

File selected…

Loading…

{ERROR CODE 79}

Reloading…

Audio-visual player standing by…

Buffering…

System ready…

Press [PLAY] to activate…

Vlogger 1 (Female – approximate age 10 years – approximate height 130cm – light brown hair):
Is it working now? *she approaches the recording device and her face fills the screen, showing a scattering of amber freckles across her nose and upper cheeks. The footage jumps as though the device is being shaken and several loud thumps reverberate through the speaker*

Vlogger 2 (Male – approximate age 10 years – approximate height 128cm – ginger hair):
It won't be for long if you keep hitting it like that.

Vlogger 1:
Well, one of us has to do something – we don't have much time. Check it again.

Vlogger 2:
huffs It's recording, OK? Let's get on with it. Wait – what are you doing?

Vlogger 1:
I'm plaiting my hair, obviously. These people are seeing me for the first time – I want to get my look right. I'm thinking Katniss plait, with a few strands

coming loose to show I've been running for my life.

Vlogger 2:
But they can see you doing it, Lottie! They know you're just sitting on a chair in my bedroom. Anyway, it doesn't matter what you look like. *sighs loudly*

Vlogger 1 (Lottie):
That's an unhelpful comment, Mo, and I am going to ignore it. Now, pause the recording while I find a hairband.

Mo sighs again, slides off his chair and stomps over to the camera. A streak of dirt can be seen down the left side of his nose. A click can be heard and the recording pauses
a second click. Mo mutters a word which sounds like it could be a swear, though it is too quiet to be sure

Mo:
Can we get on…?

Lottie:

I'll start, shall I? Good. First, I will state my name for the recording. I am Lottie Magnolia Button. And this is…

Mo:

Mo.

Lottie:

Do it properly, Mo! They're not going to be able to identify your burnt remains if they only know you as Mo. Our lives could depend on this.

Mo:

Fine. Morris Albert Appleby.

Lottie:

Albert? Really? And I thought Morris was questionable.

Mo:

Are you serious? Your middle name is Magnolia. MAGNOLIA. What even is that?

Lottie:

It's a flower: beautiful but tough. Everyone knows

that. Honestly, who would have thought that you, Mo Appleby, are destined to be one of the saviours of man and womankind?

Mo:
Just get on with it, Lottie – we don't know how much time we have before…

Lottie:
…They find us. You're right. OK, this is a message – a terribly important message. If you are watching this message…

Mo:
They're probably going to stop watching if you say 'message' one more time.

Lottie:
If you are watching this MESSAGE, then it means something has happened to us and the future of the world is in your hands.

Mo:
We can't tell our parents because they won't believe us.

Lottie:

And we can't tell the police because we don't know who we can trust.

Mo:

Anybody could be one of them. Anybody could be a Junker.

Lottie:

And if you're watching this then it means they got us. We're probably dead.

Mo:

We're probably NOT dead. But we might have been junked, and that's almost as bad.

Lottie:

And I am ever so important, dear viewer. The world needs me. And Mo.

Mo:

Especially Mo.

Lottie:

So please keep watching and you'll understand

everything. I'm going to explain – to tell you our story…

Mo:
No, I'm going to tell the story, Lottie. You'll tell it wrong.

Lottie:
No way, Mo, you'll tell it boringly.

Mo *sighs*:
If by boringly, you mean truthfully, then yes I will.

Lottie:
It's my story as much as yours, Mo. I don't see why you should get to tell it.

Mo:
Shall we just take it in turns, then?

Lottie:
OK – I'll go first.

Mo:
No, I'll go first – the story starts with me.

Lottie:

Only technically.

Mo:

Right. Only technically, rather than in your imagination.

Lottie:

So, anyway, courageous viewer: please hear our story and take action. You might be our only chance for survival. And hurry – maybe there's still time. Maybe you can save us.

The Start of the Story

Mo

'Hurry up, Mo – they're here!' Mum called to me from the empty hallway.

'I'm doing a check,' I said, standing in what used to be my bedroom at 79 Morello Road, but was now just a room waiting to belong to someone who wasn't me.

'Just one more, my love. I know it's hard to say goodbye, but we really have to go. We've got a new adventure ahead of us.'

After ten perfect years of just me, Mum and our cat, Schrodinger, the time had come for us to become part of a new 'family'. We were leaving our house – the one I'd lived in since I was born; the one I knew as well as I knew myself – and moving into a house across the street. Even worse, we were going to be living with Mum's – I don't want to say boyfriend, because, one: she's too old to have a boyfriend; and two: it's gross – we were going to be living with Mum's Spencer, and his daughters, Lottie and Sadie. I could talk for hours about how this was the worst thing that had happened in my life, but Lottie will use it as an excuse to interrupt, so I'll just say that I wasn't happy about it.

But Mum was. And my mum is the kindest, coolest, most awesome mum in the world. She has a smile that fills her whole face and she always smells like pancakes and strawberries. My dad disappeared before I was born; before Mum even knew she was having me. He just walked out one day and never came back. That made her sad for a long time. Not sad the whole time, but there were moments. Like when I was having trouble with some kids at school and my teacher called her in. She said she wished my dad was there to help us. And when we went on holiday, I could see her looking around, hoping she might see him. But then she met Spencer, and those moments happened less often.

Before I said goodbye, I had to complete one last check – to make sure I wasn't leaving anything important. I knelt on the floorboards and crawled slowly across the room, back and forth until I'd covered every centimetre. My carpet had been worn out and torn in one corner where Schrodinger had scratched at it, so Mum thought it was best to pull it up and throw it out. The room looked so different without it. There were gaps between the wooden planks and I was worried that I might have dropped something; that something tiny might get left behind.

And that's when I found the loose one. In the cat-clawed corner, one of the boards wobbled when I knelt on it. Through the crack at the edge, I could see something shining in the darkness underneath – a dull, silver colour. I squidged my fingers under the board and pulled.

Lottie

Sadie and I were desperate to see our new room, but Dad wouldn't let us go into the house until the others arrived. So we stood outside 124 Morello Road – a big white house, with lots of wide windows, that stood out amongst the narrow brown brick houses surrounding it. It was at the top of the hill and set back from the road, up some steep steps, so it was higher and bolder and looked more important than the other houses on the street. It gave me the impression that it was keeping a lookout over Morello Road. We waited by the door while the peculiar ginger boy, who was going to be our new brother, and the pretty ginger lady, who was going to be our new mother, had an intense discussion in the doorway of their old house, which happened to be opposite our new house.

I couldn't hear what they were saying, but it ended with the boy waiting until his mum had turned her back and then putting something shiny grey into his pocket.

'Hello again, girls – lovely to see you, as always! Isn't this exciting?' Our new mother smiled at us while Dad put his arm around her and kissed her (on the lips), which I still hadn't got used to. 'You remember Mo,' she said.

'Hi, Mo,' I said.

'Hi,' said Mo, looking at me as though he wished I was dead.

'Sadie, say hello,' Dad said, pulling on one of her little pigtails.

'Mew,' said Sadie, which is her way of saying hello.

'Try to use your words, Sadie,' said Dad. 'Emma and Mo can't understand you like Lottie and I can.'

'It's OK, we've got plenty of time to get to know each other,' Emma gave Sadie a bag of chocolate buttons. 'Say hello to Sadie, Mo.'

'Hello to Sadie,' Mo said, looking at Sadie as if he wished she was dead.

'Let's do it, shall we?' Dad said, putting the key in the lock of our new front door.

'Yay!' Emma laughed and clapped her hands.

Sadie munched on her buttons.

Mo kicked his shoes against the steps.

'Pineapple,' I said, to fill the silence and because it seemed appropriate.

We walked into the house.

Too Much Stuff

Lottie

After spending a million hours unpacking, it became clear that we all had a lot of stuff and not enough places to put it. This was especially relevant in Mo's case because he had mountains of full cardboard boxes that he mysteriously referred to as 'his collection'.

'We're going to have to store some of it in the garage,' Dad said. 'Would that be OK with you, Mo? I know your collection is important to you.'

I didn't like the way Dad was being all careful around Mo, but apparently he's a hashtag 'sensitive boy' and we had to be hashtag 'extra considerate'. If it had been mine or Sadie's belongings that were overflowing out of the house, we would have just been told they were getting dumped in the garage, no arguments.

Mo looked panicky.

'We just can't fit everything in, Mo-Bear,' Emma said, kneeling down and holding his hand. 'It'll be safe in the garage.'

'We could all do with a bit of stream-lining,' said Dad, 'Especially with our non-essential items. How about we all get one box each that we can fill and keep in our rooms, and everything else goes into the garage?'

'Well that sounds very fair, doesn't it, Mo?' Emma said, smiling at my dad like he was some kind of brilliant and wondrous genius. 'I have lots of things I don't really need in the house, so I'll do it too.'

'My box needs to be private,' said Mo. 'No-one's allowed to go in it.'

'We'll all have a secret box – out of bounds to everyone else. How does that sound?' Emma said, giving Mo a Curly Wurly.

'Great,' Dad said.

'Mrow,' Sadie said, which meant she agreed.

'Huff,' Mo said.

'I promise never to look in anyone's box,' I said, crossing my fingers in my head, rather than behind my back, in case anyone saw.

Mo

How could this house be so much bigger, but feel so much smaller than our old home?

The thing about me is that I collect junk. No, wait – that's not quite right: I collect items that other people might mistakenly call junk. Things that have been dropped or forgotten: the bits of paper that fall out of pockets; the random shoe from the middle of the road; the half-bald teddy lying next to the swings. It isn't that I want the things for myself – I'm not weird or anything. It's just that I can't stand to see things left behind.

I know what the other kids say about me. They think because I don't say anything back that I can't hear them laughing when I stash a soggy mitten in my bag. I do hear them, but I don't care. I can't just leave it there, drowning in a puddle, when to somebody somewhere it could be the most important mitten in the world.

Nobody and nothing is junk. Every item has a story, and a home, and probably someone missing it.

For as long as I can remember, I've collected stuff and kept it all in labelled boxes that I stored in the house. But, apparently, now that I had sisters, I had to try harder to share. And that included my space.

I filled my box, leaving just enough space for the thing I found under the floorboard. As I put the lid on, Lottie walked into my room, without knocking, and sat on my bed. *She sat on my bed.*

Her hair was brown and curly and she'd worn it a different way every time I'd seen her. Like she actually spent her time thinking up a different hairstyle for each day of the week. That's just mental. Her freckles and eyes were the colour of honey – full of sugar and sunshine. They were probably the prettiest eyes I'd ever seen. I didn't like them one bit.

'I don't like you calling my mum "Emma",' I said. 'It sounds weird.'

'Then what do you suggest?'

'How about "Miss Appleby"?'

'That's absolutely ridiculous,' Lottie said. 'She isn't my teacher. How about I call her "Mum"?'

It was the most horrible thing I'd ever heard. '"Emma" is fine.'

'I'm glad we have that settled.' She looked around my room, making a face. 'But while we're on the subject of names, you've been saying Sadie's completely wrong and she's finding it quite upsetting.'

'How have I been saying it wrong?'

'You pronounce it like "Say-dee", not "Say-dee".'

What the heck? 'You just said it the exact same way twice!'

'You obviously weren't listening properly.'

'Maybe you weren't speaking properly,' I said. I didn't really know how to deal with someone so unhinged.

'It must be all that…interesting hair blocking your ear-holes.'

'What do you mean, "interesting hair"?'

'I've never seen anything like it in my life. You know you could wear it a different way?'

'A different way?' What was she on about?

'Yes, something less Victorian street urchin and more, you know, nice. I could style it for you, if you like?' She stood up and started coming towards me.

'Hell, no.'

'There's no need for the inappropriate language, Mo. I was only trying to help.'

'I don't need your help.'

'Maybe you don't, but your hair certainly does.'

'Who even cares about hair? It doesn't matter!'

Lottie gasped. 'Take that back.'

'Hair is stupid, hair is stupid, hair is stupid,' I started chanting and marching around the room, waving my arms in the air.

Lottie

His hair was bright orange, which was fine. The problem was the way he wore it, like he'd never brushed it in his life. And he always had dirty fingers that he scratched his nose with, leaving black smudges on his face. He looked like he should be picking pockets or sweeping chimneys. It bothered me. And you know those dogs who have huge chocolatey-brown eyes, which always look sad? Well, Mo's eyes were like that, but they were dark blue. Blue eyes are supposed to be twinkly, cheerful and always look like their owner has something up their sleeves. Sad blue eyes are not a thing. Unless your name is Mo Appleby, apparently. And the worst thing was that they were ever so endearing – they made me want to share my cookies with him. It was extremely irritating.

And I don't even know where to start with his clothes. They should have been mismatched and holey, but instead they were cool and really brought out the forlornness in his face. I suspected his mum chose them for him.

'What have you put in your box?' I asked.

'That's private,' he said, putting his hand on the

lid like I was going to try to look inside. As if I'd be stupid enough to attempt it right in front of his face. 'What have you put in yours?'

'A hair from the tail of a unicorn. He gave it to me to thank me for saving his life.'

'Right,' Mo said.

Sadie walked in carrying a fat, orange cat under her arm like a handbag.

'What are you doing in here?' Mo said, looking outraged. 'And what are you doing with Schrodinger?'

'Perow meow prew,' Sadie said.

Mo just looked at her.

'Preowt.'

'What is she doing in here? What is she doing with my cat? And why does she talk in that way?' Mo turned to me, bright red in his plump cheeks.

'She came to see what you put in your box, obviously,' I rolled my eyes. 'Also, Schrodinger is a stupid name. Let's call him Tiger instead, and get him a stripey jacket.'

'Let's not,' he said.

'And Sadie was just starting to talk when Mum left. Meow was her first word. She's saving all her other words until Mum comes back for us.'

'Where's your mum gone?'

'She's on a top-secret archeological dig. As a matter of fact, she's discovered the fossil of a dinosaur that nobody's ever found before. She's calling it the LottieSadieSaurus. She'll come for us when her work is done.'

'Why didn't she take you with her?' Mo asked. (I discovered early on that he is not very tactful.)

'No schools in the Sahara,' I said.

'Right,' said Mo.

Mo

I had two strange girls in my bedroom.

One of them was throwing stuff out of my drawers while cuddling my cat like he was a teddy bear. He seemed to like it, too, which was so annoying. The other girl was asking rude questions and telling me stories about her mum that I wasn't a hundred per cent sure were true. What had my life become?

'We always wanted a brother,' Lottie said. 'You're not quite what we imagined, but you'll have to do.'

'What did you imagine?'

'Less short, less ginger.' Lottie put her hands on her hips.

'Eroww,' Sadie said.

'Sadie, you shouldn't call people chubby,' Lottie said.

'Rowwr.'

'Yes, even if they are. And that hat doesn't suit Tiger – try the green one.'

How offensive! 'Really? Well, I never wanted one sister, never mind two. And stop putting hats on my cat!'

'That's OK. I'm sure you were much too busy putting things in alphabetical order to think about the joy of sisters. We must be a fabulous surprise for you. And how dare you try to take Tiger's hat from him when it makes him look like a white-hot fashionista?'

My room was in a state. They were out of control, like a whirlwind. They were a girlwind. Just then the doorbell rang and they ran off, leaving me to wonder what a white-hot fashionista was.

Lottie

Our new front door has some of that cloudy glass in it, so you can see a deformed reflection of whoever is on the other side.

As we reached the bottom of the stairs, I could see the outline of a small woman with long, bouncy hair. For a second I thought it was Mum – that she'd come back for us at last. But as I pulled open the door, it wasn't Mum's face I saw.

There was a stranger there. At first I thought she was young and extraordinarily beautiful, but when I looked again, I changed my mind. She had masses of shiny blonde hair that went all the way down her back. I'd never have thought it was possible to have too much hair, but somehow she managed it. And there was something off about the colour – it didn't go with her skin or her eyes. Her face wasn't right either. It looked like her skin was stretched almost too tight over her cheeks, and her neck looked a bit crinkly. My nana has a crinkly neck, and it looks lovely, but on this woman, with her tight face, it was all wrong.

'Oh,' I said, feeling like I might cry.

'Good afternoon, sweet girls,' the lady smiled, looking over my shoulder and down the hallway behind me. 'Have you just moved in? Could I perhaps have a little chat with your mother and father?'

'Prow,' Sadie said and walked off into the living room.

'Did the removal truck and boxes give it away?' I said, annoyed that I could have thought for a second that this woman was my mum.

'What a cherub you are!' She clapped her hands. 'Just delightful! Now, angel, – your mother and father?'

'Mother! Father!' I called. 'There's someone at the door for you.'

'I'll just step inside, shall I?' the woman said, peering into the boxes in the hall as Emma and Dad came out of the kitchen. 'Ah! There you are, at last. I came to introduce myself – I'm your new neighbour, Lorelai. I'm sure we're going to be great friends.'

'Hello,' said Emma. 'Lovely to meet you. I'd offer you a coffee but we've not unpacked the kettle yet.' Emma and Dad laughed, but Lorelai just stared at them.

'I've just moved in myself across the road,' Lorelai said. 'And I don't even have a kettle, so I'm happy to wait while you look for yours.'

'Oh, right, of course,' Emma said, while Dad gave her a look. 'You'd better come in.'

'While you're looking, you couldn't be a doll and loan me some sugar, could you?' Lorelai walked past Emma, towards the kitchen.

Emma raised an eyebrow at Dad who shook his head.

'No problem,' Emma said. 'Please make yourself at home.'

'I think she already has,' Dad whispered to me as he followed them into the kitchen.

Rather than listening to whatever boring conversation they'd be having, I went to find Sadie.

St Pippins Primary

Mo

The shiny lady didn't leave until dinnertime. Even though she'd only just moved in to my lovely old house, there were no vans parked outside or boxes in sight and she said she didn't have anything to do. It seemed strange – our house was chaotic, there was stuff everywhere. When I peeped over at number 79, the only thing that looked different was that all the curtains were closed. I kept sneaking peeks all weekend, to try to catch a glimpse inside, but the curtains stayed shut all day and all night. It was the same when we left for school on Monday.

'It was nice of Emma to force you to show me the way to school,' Lottie said the next morning, as we reached the zebra crossing in front of the gates.

'Mum is always nice,' I said, picking up a loom bracelet that was about to fall down a drain. 'She probably put a chocolate muffin in your schoolbag, too.'

'That probably has germs,' Lottie said, wrinkling her nose at the bracelet. 'But, yay! Muffin!' She started fiddling around in her bag and nearly stepped into the road without looking.

'Watch out. We have to wait until the lollipop man says we can cross.'

'You have a lollipop man? How adorable! I thought that only happened in historical school dramas.'

The lollipop man dropped his stick and stared at us from the pavement opposite.

'What's his name?' she asked.

'I don't know.' I peered at the small part of his face that wasn't covered by his neon hat, which was pulled down low, almost over his eyes. 'It isn't Derek, the old lollipop man. This one must be new.'

'He's quite starey, isn't he?' Lottie said.

The lollipop man suddenly stepped out into the road, without even looking at the traffic. His stick was on the floor, so none of the drivers saw him coming. Cars came skidding to a halt. Horns beeped loudly. Drivers shouted out of their windows. Finger swears were thrown around like it was a 12A movie. He didn't even look at them, just carried on staring at us.

'You need to pick up the stick!' Lottie shouted at him.

'Let's just cross,' I said. We were attracting far too much attention, and I really prefer to keep a low profile at school.

'He's probably going to be fired by the end of the day,' Lottie said, as we made it safely to the other side of the road and the traffic started moving again.

I watched him picking up his stick while kids and their parents laughed behind their hands at him. He looked a bit lost, sort of out of place. I felt sorry for him so I turned back and gave him a smile and a thumbs-up.

He winked at me.

Lottie

I don't know why Emma thought Mo would be able to help me settle in at school. I'd been there five minutes and I could already tell that he was the type of kid who pretended to be sick at lunchtime so he could spend the hour alone in the medical room, reading. He didn't seem to have any friends. Of course, I didn't either, but that didn't bother me at all. Other people have always gravitated towards me – I think it's because of my vibrant aura.

It was a small school and, as there was only a month between mine and Mo's birthdays, we were in the same class.

'Anyone not in a group for the Discovery Day Competition yet?' Mr Chartwell, our teacher, said, on my first morning at St Pippins.

Mo put his hand up and looked at the desk.

I felt rather sorry for him. Yes, he was strange and grumpy, enjoyed picking up trash from the street and had a terrible attitude to hair, but he wasn't all bad. Besides, everybody should have a friend.

'May I work with Mo?' I asked.

Mr Chartwell smiled. Mo looked surprised. 'Yes, of course, Lottie. I'm passing round a handout with the competition details – have a read through and then you can all start brainstorming.'

At this point, I'd like to refer you to Exhibit A from the evidence box:

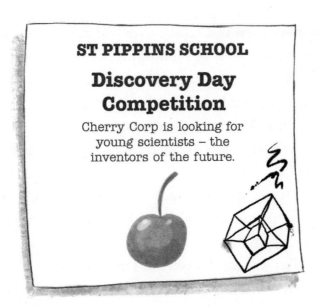

ST PIPPINS SCHOOL

Discovery Day Competition

Cherry Corp is looking for young scientists – the inventors of the future.

Mo turned to me while I read through the handout. 'Before we start, Lottie, there's something I want to say...'

'It's OK, Mo, you don't have to thank me for working with you. You're basically my brother, after all.'

'No, I was going to say that this competition is really important. In case you didn't know, my dad was an important biomedical engineer...'

'A what?'

'He was a brilliant scientist and I want to be just as good as him. I need to win this competition, so

I don't want you taking over and ruining it. It's probably best if you follow my instructions very carefully at every stage, or just watch and let me do everything.'

'Well, that's rude and ungrateful.'

'I thought you just said I didn't have to thank you!'

'Of course I said that, Morris, because THAT is what people say in these kinds of situations. Everybody knows that.'

'But why say it if you don't mean it?'

We were interrupted by a boy with straight, black hair and shifty eyes who slumped himself down in the chair next to us. 'I'm new. The teacher said I have to work with you.'

'I'm new, too,' I said, giving him my most dazzling smile. If he was on our team, I wanted him to be on my side. 'I'm Lottie, this is Mo. What's your name?'

'It's Jax,' he said.

The New Boy

Lottie, who has been fidgeting for the past few minutes, starts to jiggle urgently on her chair

Lottie:
Mo, I need a wee.

Mo:
Go then. What do you want? My permission?

Lottie:
I want you to come with me.

Mo:
Gross.

Lottie:
And wait outside the door, I mean.

Mo:
Why?

Lottie:

I'm scared the Junkers will come while I'm tinkling.

Mo:

You are not. You just don't trust me with the vlog on my own. But you're going to have to either trust me or wet yourself, because there is no way I'm coming to the toilet with you.

Lottie:

Fine. I can hold it.

She crosses her legs, jiggles for another second, and then jumps to her feet

Lottie:

I can't hold it! Don't say anything about me while I'm gone!

She runs out of the room
Mo moves close to the camera

Mo *whispering*:

Before we carry on with the story, I should just warn you not to believe everything Lottie says.

She's not a liar, exactly – well, mostly she's not a liar – but she does exaggerate A LOT. Just keep that in mind.

Footsteps can be heard, quietly at first, but growing louder, and Lottie runs into the room

Lottie *out of breath*:
I'm back.

Mo:
You didn't wash your hands.

Lottie:
This is an emergency situation: normal rules don't apply. Everyone knows that.

Mo:
Gross.

Lottie grabs at Mo

Mo:
Get off me, Lottie! I don't want you to touch me with your wee fingers.

Lottie *laughs wildly*:
Serves you right for not coming with me. Now you are covered in my wee residue.

Mo:
I hate you.

Lottie:
Now where was I?

Mo:
I'm doing the next bit – you've been talking for ages.

Lottie *sighs*:
Fine, if it will stop you from being in a mood.

Mo
The new boy snatched the handout and started doodling on it with black pen. And, by doodling, I mean he drew all over my epically important competition poster. And, by black pen, I mean he used unerasable ink.

If you take a look at Exhibit A from the evidence box, you will see the doodle in its original form. It's in the bottom, right corner of the handout.

'If you want to win this dumb competition,' he said, smudging his doodle with his sleeve, 'I should lead the group. Science is my thing.'

Lottie raised an eyebrow at me. 'Ooh,' she said.

'What?' Jax looked up from his mindless graffiti.

'Well,' Lottie said, apparently all excited at the disaster unfolding in front of her. 'It's just that…'

'Science is *my* thing,' I said, taking the pen out of Jax's hand and putting it firmly down on the desk.

Jax looked from me to Lottie and back again.

'Hey, no problem, bud, I was just trying to help. You can take charge,' he said.

I felt a bit bad.

'No, no, it's fine. You should take charge,' I said, hoping he'd refuse and insist that I did.

'Why don't we all just work as a team?' Lottie said. 'Agreed?'

'Agreed,' said Jax.

'Agreed,' I said, but I snuck the pen into my pocket, just in case.

She'd only been at school for a day, but it was like Lottie had spent her whole life at St Pippins. By first break, she was chatting with a group of girls from my class. By lunchtime, she was their leader – bossing them around, getting them to plait her hair and making them all laugh hysterically whenever she said anything. Worse than that, even the boys liked her. When a ball was kicked out of the MUGA, she dribbled it back in, took it past three of the kids from the school football team, and scored a goal. You should have seen the respect on their faces. I've known them for seven years, and they've never looked at me like that.

I wasn't jealous, exactly. I'd never wanted to be friends with any of them anyway. But I was annoyed.

'I thought you two were friends,' Jax said, sitting on the wall of the vegetable patch next to me.

'We're NOT friends,' I said. 'My mum is going out with Lottie's dad, so we all live together.'

Jax gave me a sharp look. 'Like brother and sister, then?'

'No. Not like that, either.'

'Your name is Mo, right?'

'Yes,' I said. 'And you'd probably better not talk to me if you want to be one of the popular kids.' It was only fair to warn him, after all.

Jax flicked his hair back from his face. 'You know, I've never been bothered about the popular kids.'

I looked across at him, wondering if he was trying to trick me.

He smiled suddenly – a quick, bright smile that cracked across his face like a flash of lightning. 'Do you want to work on ideas for the Discovery Competition?'

'Yeah, sure,' I said, trying to play it cool while feeling a warm glow in my heart.

'If we come up with ideas while Lottie is busy with her friends, she'll have to go along with what we want.'

'She's very stubborn,' I said.

'But then it will be us against her,' Jax watched my face. 'Why should she always get her own way? Science is *your* thing, remember?'

'So, you want to team up with me? Against Lottie?'

'Partners?' Jax said, holding out his hand.

'Partners,' I nodded, and shook it.

'So, tell me more about what you like doing, Mo. Maybe we could come up with an idea to do with your interests,' Jax said, offering me a gummy worm from a bag he had hidden in his pocket.

'Sweets aren't allowed at school,' I said, thinking it was something else he hadn't realised because of his newness.

'Nobody has to know.' He bit the head off an orange one.

A Warning

Lottie

Mo didn't seem to want me around at playtime, so I had to hang out with some of the other kids from my class. At lunchtime, I collected my tray from the dinner lady and looked around for Mo. He was still in the lunch queue, waiting for his chicken sausages and spicy wedges, a little way back from the rest of the class, on his own like always. I really did feel sorry for him. I sat down at a table and kept a spare seat next to me, so he could sit with me, but instead he walked to the back of the hall and sat with a bunch of year one kids who threw peas at him. My table soon filled up with girls from my class, so I chatted to them while I ate.

I tried again to talk to him when we were putting our trays away, but he hurried off while I was scraping the beans off my plate. I started to call after him, but then I noticed a folded-up piece of paper stuck to the bottom of my plate. I looked around, but nobody was watching me and giggling, like they were pranking me. A secret note! I was rather excited, so I opened it immediately. I expected it to be a letter from an admirer telling me that they had fallen madly in love with me. But it wasn't a love letter.

I'd now like you to look at Exhibit B – aka The First Note Of Destiny:

> **YOU ARE IN GREAT DANGER!**
> **DO NOT TRUST ANYBODY!**
> **PEOPLE ARE NOT WHAT THEY SEEM!**
> **THE JUNKERS COULD BE ANYWHERE!!**

My first thought was that there was a rather thrilling use of multiple exclamation marks. My second thought was that I had no clue what 'Junkers' were, but they sounded dirty. My third thought was that I wanted to show Mo.

A bunch of girls dragged me into their game. Not knowing who was a true friend, I played and laughed along, keeping an eye open for Mo. Finally, one of the boys kicked a ball out of the MUGA, so I made a big show of running around with it, so that I could look for him at the other side of the playground.

At last, I found him, sitting on a wall and chatting away to Jax. He wouldn't talk to me, but he would talk to the doodler? I was deeply offended.

From the moment I met Jax, I didn't like him. He was strange and arrogant and he didn't seem to care what I thought of him. It was completely unacceptable. And there he was, buddying up with Mo while stuffing his face with forbidden sweets. Mo must have noticed them, because I saw his face change suddenly, as he said something to Jax.

'Now you're for it,' I said, waiting for the argument that would end with Mo stomping off to be on his own. Mo doesn't like people who break the rules.

But then I saw Mo smile, take a sweet and put it in his mouth. Just like that, he had turned to a life of crime. I didn't know what I was most annoyed about: that Jax hadn't offered me his illegal sweets instead of Mo; or that Mo had gone over to the dark side for Jax when he would never do anything even slightly risky with me. Mo had only known Jax for about two seconds, while we were practically family. It was exceptionally infuriating and it made me wonder if I knew him at all.

If the note was a trick, who had sent it? And if the note was real, my life was in danger. Either way, I didn't know who I could trust. And that included Mo.

'Mo and I have decided we want to invent some kind of reuniting device,' Jax said, showing me some diagrams he and Mo had been working on behind my back.

'Why?'

'Because Mo has a collection of things he's found and he wants to get them back to their owners.'

'And we've done some research here at school and the lost-property situation is getting out of hand,' Mo said.

'The school office has been overwhelmed with items that have been left over the years,' Jax added.

'So we will design a solution to this problem.' Mo said, in a voice that sounded like he'd been practising his lines.

'Sounds boring,' I said. 'We need to think of something with more wow.'

'Two votes to one,' Jax said, giving Mo a secret smile. 'And we have good news: the Head has given us permission to go through lost property to help us with our invention.'

He wiggled a bunch of keys in my face.

We went to the lost-property cupboard, which was basically a small room, with shelves on the walls, cupboards and drawers and piles and piles of stuff.

'Do we not need some kind of plan of what we're actually going to make, before we look through these mouldy old things?' I said.

'We have to be methodical, Lottie,' Mo said. 'We'll go through and document each item and put the information into a database.'

'Inventions are supposed to be exciting,' I said.

'Inventions are supposed to be useful,' Mo huffed.

'Let's just get looking, shall we?' Jax was already rooting through a heap of rags.

'Are you looking for something specific, Jax?' I said.

'Of course not,' he said, without glancing up. 'Just thought it might trigger some more ideas.'

'Maybe we should do it in a particular order...' Mo said, looking worried as Jax threw old school jumpers everywhere.

Honestly, Jax was going a bit crazy, opening boxes and tipping them out all over the floor. It was Mo's idea of a nightmare. I have no problem with mess, but to me it seemed suspicious, like he had an ulterior motive.

'I'll start making notes, then.' Mo opened his notebook.

'Ugh, this tie is covered in hair,' I said, dropping my bundle in disgust.

'That's it!' said Mo. 'DNA!'

'What?' I asked, as Jax ignored both of us and kept digging.

'We can design a system to locate the owners of items using DNA. All these items have hair, or skin flakes or bodily fluids on them. We'll run forensic tests!'

'First, that's gross,' I said. 'And second, we only have a couple of weeks until our inventions have to be ready. That sounds like it's going to take years of dull, boring work.'

'But it's brilliant,' Mo said, 'We can get all these items, and the ones in my collection, back where they belong.'

'It's not exciting and it's not going to work,' I said. 'What do you think, Jax?'

'What Mo said.' Jax picked up a box and shook it. He smiled when it rattled and ripped it open.

'I'll get some specimen jars and labels,' Mo said, running off all excited.

I watched Jax rummaging around in a box and I wondered about my note. I'd only just joined the school, and I didn't know where to start looking, either for the person who sent it to me, or for these Junkers it was warning me about.

I sat on a stack of old books and started flicking through a load of dusty class photos. They all had dates on them – I even found one from 1989, which was basically like Victorian times.

That's when I came across my first clue. It was a class photo, from ten years ago. I glanced at the smiling faces of the children and noticed one face that wasn't smiling. Take a look: Exhibit E – front row, three from the right. The miserable boy in the picture had the same straight, floppy black hair as the boy who was right in front of me, emptying the pockets of old school shorts. And even more shockingly, he had the exact same face. It was impossible, but the boy in the Year 6 photo from ten years ago was identical to Jax.

Mo

When I ran back into the storage room, Lottie was stuffing something into her pocket.

'What was that?' I said.

'A tissue,' she said, 'I have a dreadful cold.'

It was not a tissue and she didn't have a cold. I didn't know why she was lying to me, but it made me even more determined not to talk to her. Unfortunately, I'd promised Mum we'd walk home together.

We heard the screech of tyres and angry voices before we even got to the gates. A crowd had gathered at the crossing, surrounding this kid called Leo who was sitting at the side of the road, while his mum yelled at the lollipop man.

'He could have been killed!' she screamed, pulling Leo up by his arm and dusting him down so ferociously that he backed away from her.

'You see! He's terrified!'

'Ah, I do apologise,' the lollipop man said. 'First day on the job and I'm still getting used to this stick thingy.' He waggled his lollipop.

'His scooter's broken! HIS SCOOTER'S BROKEN!' She pointed at Leo's scooter which had obviously gone under the wheel of a car. It was one of those black shiny ones, with lights that came on when you were going fast. I knew this because he drove it into the backs of my feet pretty much every day on the way into school. It was badly bent and the front wheel was half off.

'Ooo,' Lottie said. 'That boy's scooter's broken.'

'Hooray,' I said, smiling at the thought of walking to school without the skin being scraped off my heels. 'That lollipop man's done us a favour.'

'It's not completely broken,' the lollipop man said, picking it up. 'Look – it works!' He got on it and tried to scoot around in the road. The lights on one side flickered and then went out completely and the front wheel popped off and rolled away.

Leo's mum got her phone out. 'I'm taking pictures and reporting you to the council!' She pointed it towards the lollipop man.

'That's out of the question,' he said, pulling his hat down even further over his face. 'No pictures. If you don't put that phone away, I'll have to take it.'

'You're a psycho,' she said. 'You shouldn't be working near our little ones.'

'Ooh,' said Lottie, who was enjoying herself a weirdly large amount.

'What's your name? I'm going to write a letter to the school governors!' Leo's mum shrieked.

'You're free to cross, now,' he said, turning his back on her.

'Not until I have your name!'

'It's Hector. Now get off my crossing.'

The crowd went off in their separate directions and Lottie and I reached the kerb.

'This lollipop man is a liability,' Lottie said, as he straightened his yellow coat. He walked into the road, one hand holding his stick and the other in his pocket, which was so full it was bulging.

'I wonder what he has in his pocket,' I said.

'Probably the bones of the children who've been run over on his crossing,' Lottie said. 'Or mouse brains.'

'Why would he have mouse brains?' She was absolutely mental.

'More importantly, why would he wear yellow when it does nothing for his complexion?' Lottie said. 'He'd look much better in a cobalt blue.'

'It's a uniform,' I said. 'I don't think he got to choose.'

Hector looked over at us from the middle of the road and frowned.

'I think he heard you again, Lottie,' I whispered. 'Why do you always have to be rude so loudly?'

'I'm not going to be rude quietly, am I?' she said. 'That's a much worse way of being rude. Everyone knows that.'

Hector nodded for all the people waiting on the pavement to cross, but he looked only at us. When we reached where he stood in the middle of the crossing, he suddenly reached out a hand and grabbed me.

'The Discovery Competition,' he said. 'You must win. The future depends on it.'

'Oh, er, I'll try?' I said, wriggling myself out of his grasp.

'You must succeed.' He pulled me closer to him and looked right into my eyes. Then he let me go.

'What was that about?' I said to Lottie when

we'd made it over the road to safety. 'It was kind of creepy.'

'It was extremely creepy,' she said. 'And even worse, he touched you with his mouse brain hand. Now you've got mouse brain on your sleeve.' She started laughing.

I rubbed my sleeve on her face.

Lorelai and the Thief

Lottie

As we walked up to the house, the woman from across the road was coming out of our front door, buttoning up her jacket. She was smiling fakely, showing rows of teeth, which looked too bright and too straight to be real. They practically glinted in the sun. When she spotted Mo and I, just for a second, her smile turned into more of a silent snarl, which was surprising since all we were doing was walking up the steps to our own front door.

'Did I do something?' Mo whispered. 'Is my face offensive?'

'No more than usual,' I said. 'I don't know what her problem is.'

'Mo-Bear! Lottie! How was your day?' Emma said from the doorway. 'You remember Mrs... Oh, I'm so sorry – I can't remember your last name?'

'Lorelai is fine,' the woman beamed back at Emma.

'Why are your curtains always closed?' Mo said.

Lorelai laughed and flicked her glossy hair behind her shoulder.

'Did I say something funny?' Poor Mo looked very confused. His freckly cheeks had turned bright pink.

'Oh, bless you, lovely observant little boy!' Lorelai reached out as though she was going to pat him on the head or something, but pulled her hand back at the last moment, as though she found him too disgusting.

'She must know about the mouse brains,' I said.

Mo nodded.

'So why do you keep the curtains closed, Rapunz… I mean, Lorelai?' I asked.

She ran her tongue across her top teeth, 'There's a very good reason, actually. Don't worry, I'm not a vampire,' she laughed.

Mo looked uncomfortable.

'I've just decorated and bought new furniture.'

'Really?' I said. 'That was quick.'

'Thank you, angel,' she said, though I don't know what she was thanking me for. I didn't mean it as a compliment. 'The sun is so bright at the front of the house, and you know it makes colours fade if it shines on something too much.

54

So I keep the curtains closed to protect my lovely things. Having a beautiful home is so important to me.'

'Mewl perowt err,' Sadie said, which meant 'it would be more believable if she told us she really was a vampire – what a bunch of …'

'Absolutely,' I nodded.

Mo just squinted at her and wrinkled his nose.

'Come on in then, you two – I want to hear all about your day,' Emma gave us both a squeeze as Lorelai walked down the steps waving goodbye.

'So wonderful to see you again, darling Emma,' she half sang, as though she was a Disney princess, 'And thank you for the cookies – I'll be sure to pay you back.'

'Yes, you too, and no problem at all – do let me know if you need anything else – it must be tough to manage alone when you've just moved in and don't know the area.'

'Yes, very tough, but I know I have a friend close-by now. I'll pop over after dinner, shall I? Thank you so much! So long!'

'Let me take your bags, my lovelies. I'll get some snacks and then we can catch up.' Emma walked through to the kitchen.

'Why is she so obsessed with my mum?' Mo said, closing the front door.

'Meeeeeoooow,' said Sadie.

'Ooh, burn,' I laughed and high-fived Sadie.

Mo spun around. 'What did she say? If she said something bad about my mum, I swear, I'll...'

'You'll do what, exactly?' I said, standing between him and Sadie. 'And anyway, you're too stupid to understand Sadie, so you'll never know.'

Mo

I really wanted to be alone, but whatever room I went into, someone walked in and started talking to me. It wasn't cold out, even though it was October, so I snuck into the back garden for a relaxing bounce on my trampoline. Although I'm not a very sporty person, I have always loved my trampoline. I can block everything else out and think about stuff that makes me happy. I get my best ideas on the trampoline.

I closed my eyes and started thinking about the science competition. I loved science – it made me feel close to my dad and, when I did well, I could tell my mum was really proud. So I was desperate to win. I felt in my heart that inventing was what I was meant to do with my life. I smiled as the breeze tickled my neck and the birds chirped in the trees behind me. I breathed in the smell of grass and let the creak of the springs soothe me as I bounced. For the first time since moving, I felt calm.

Until I heard the back door crash and Lottie and Sadie came running and yelling up the garden towards me.

'Can we play with you, Mo? Let's invent a new game which involves the trampoline, a football, the rhododendron bush and this broken flowerpot.' Lottie said.

Sadie prodded her with a twig.

'And this magic twig,' Lottie added.

I cursed the day these impossible girls had come into my life. They spoke in ways I didn't understand. They did random things for no apparent reason. They made me feel stupid and stressed. Everything was hard and uncomfortable while they were around.

For example, Sadie suddenly put her hand under her T-shirt at the back and pulled something out of the back of her pants. Why? Why would someone keep something down there?

'Oh, Sadie – you haven't been at it again, have

you? Dad will go mad,' Lottie said, as she took the something, which was a folded-up piece of paper, out of Sadie's hand.

'At what again?' I asked, even though I knew I wouldn't like the answer.

'Sadie has a bit of a problem with taking things that don't belong to her,' Lottie said, looking at the piece of paper.

'You mean stealing?' I said.

'She collects things, like you do,' said Lottie.

'No, I pick up things that have been lost so I can try to get them back to their owners. That is not the same as being a thief. It's like the opposite of being a thief.'

'Don't call Sadie a thief.' Lottie turned to Sadie. 'Where did you get this, Sades?'

'Prew mew purowt.' Sadie looked down at the grass as though she felt bad, but I was pretty sure she was smiling.

'So?' I said.

'She slid it out of Lorelai's pocket while she was chatting to Emma.'

'That's really not good – we should probably give it back.'

'Do you want to knock on her door, Mo?

Because I know I don't,' said Lottie. 'Besides, it's just a piece of paper. It's worthless.'

'Let me see what's on it.' I snatched it out of her hand.

'Rude,' she said, while Sadie looked as though she was going to cry.

'It's a list of dates, times and numbers,' I said. 'The title is "Class X Occurrences Over the Past Century."

'Sounds boring,' Lottie said. 'She probably won't even notice it's gone.'

'It's weird, though… The dates start from fifty years ago, and they go up to the year 2068.'

'So?'

'So, how can there be a list of things that have happened, when the dates are in the future? You see–' I pointed at an entry, '3rd May 2026 – peak at 22:54 hrs – X 5.39.'

'It's probably just a page from a novel set in an apocalyptic future,' Lottie said, grabbing it back. 'But, just in case, you'd better get rid of it, Sades – you don't want any evidence linking you to its disappearance. Make sure you throw it away.'

Sadie nodded, folded it up and put it back down her pants.

'Hold on a sec,' I said, glaring at Sadie. 'Was it you who stole my diamond armour out of my chest in my Minecraft world?'

'Prrrrerr,' Sadie giggled.

'You horrid brat! I bet you're the one who blew up my base, too!'

'Don't shout at her like that,' Lottie shoved me. 'She took your armour and I blew up your base. Who. Even. Cares?'

'I spent three weeks building that base,' I shouted. I was so mad, I felt like I was going to explode.

'It was rubbish anyway,' Lottie rolled her eyes, 'Probably a good thing we destroyed it.'

I looked at them: the two most evil, insane and bossy girls in the whole world, and suddenly felt like I was going to cry.

'I hate you!' I said, and I ran back into the house.

Mr Gideon's
Delicious Ice Cream

Mo

Mum made us sit around the big table at dinner, which was annoying. When it was just me and her, we used to sit on the sofa with trays while Schrodinger stole food off our plates. I didn't know why we had to act all fancy just because of the new people.

Nobody spoke.

'Is the dinner OK?' Mum looked worried. 'I tried to make something everyone would like…'

'What do you call it?' Lottie said.

'Cottage pie.'

'And the green stuff is?' Lottie scooped some up on her fork and let it drop back onto the plate.

'Broccoli.'

'Really? I've never had broccoli like this before. How … interesting.'

'Sssss prowt,' Sadie said.

'Don't be so rude, girls!' Spencer gave them a very cross look.

'Grouw hsssss.'

'That language is unacceptable, Sadie.' Spencer's voice was loud and a bit shouty. 'Last warning.'

Mum looked like she might cry.

'It's lovely, Mum,' I said. 'You're the best at cooking, ever.'

'Thanks Mo-Bear.' Mum smiled at me.

Lottie sniggered.

Sadie hissed.

Spencer tutted and slammed his fork down on the plate.

'Ice cream van!' Lottie shouted, running to the front window with Sadie behind her.

Then I heard the tinkly music coming from the street.

Mum looked a bit sad, I think because of all the arguing at dinner. I felt really bad for her. 'We haven't had an ice cream van down here for years,' she said.

'Can we get one, Dad?' Lottie was jumping up and down, and Sadie held out her hand for some money.

'I don't think you've been good enough, do you?' Spencer said.

'Oh, let them get one, Spencer. It sounds like it's

been a tough day for all of them. I'm sure Mo would like one, too.'

Spencer put his arm around Mum. 'You're too lovely for your own good, you know. What did I do to deserve you?'

Mum looked a bit happier after that.

Spencer gave us some money and we legged it to the ice cream van, which was parked right outside our house.

A couple of small kids and their mums got there before us, so we had to queue. Lottie and Sadie were arguing about what ice creams to get. Apparently, they wanted to get the same, but not the same, whatever that means. I looked over at my lovely old house across the road. The curtains were shut, as usual, so I couldn't see in. It was probably a good thing because it would have made me sad.

'Mo!' Lottie shouted at me, making me jump. 'It's our turn.'

We were at the front, looking up at the ice cream man through the hatch.

'Good afternoon, sir,' Lottie said. 'What do you recommend?'

The ice cream man just stared at her. He was

probably the biggest person I'd ever seen in my life – not fat, just really wide and tall, like a wrestler. He couldn't even stand up straight in the van; he had to lean forward out of the hatch, which made him loom over us. He filled the space so I couldn't see around him.

He gave Lottie a look that suggested he didn't care what ice cream she got and he wasn't going to waste his time helping her choose.

Typically, Lottie didn't notice, though, or maybe she did but she didn't care. That's a thing I'd learnt about Lottie – she wasn't very tactful.

'Is your name Mr Gideon, or is that the name of your van?' She pointed at the sign above the hatch: Mr Gideon's Delicious Ices.

He leant further out of the hatch and spat on the road beside us.

'That's not terribly hygienic,' Lottie said.

He made a sound in the back of his throat that was a bit like a growl.

I looked down at the pool of spit and then up at Mr Gideon. He was wearing a black top with the sleeves rolled up a bit, his arms resting on the counter. The tops of his arms had bulging muscles and the lower part of his left arm was as thick as my leg. His right arm looked weird, though – it was thinner, and the hand was smaller, with longer fingers. Even the skin was a different colour – paler than the rest of him. I could see the black lines of a tattoo creeping out from under his sleeve.

Lottie nudged me, suddenly, and I looked up to see Mr Gideon staring at me in a really unfriendly way.

'Just tell him what you want,' she said. 'He doesn't talk, apparently.'

Lottie and Sadie were both licking swirly rainbow lollies.

'A cone, please, with two flakes and strawberry sauce,' I said, trying not to sound scared.

'I bet you get the same thing every time, don't you?' Lottie said, as Mr Gideon turned around to get my ice cream.

'I know what I like. There's nothing wrong with that.'

He shoved the cone towards me.

'Thank you,' I said, giving him the money.

'This is the most delicious lolly in the history of the universe,' said Lottie.

'Prrrrr,' Sadie said through a mouthful. It sounded like she agreed.

I looked at mine, tried not to think about the spit on the floor and gave it a careful lick. It was really, REALLY good.

'I'm definitely getting ice cream from Mr Gideon again,' Lottie said.

Sadie nodded.

I didn't say anything because I was too busy eating.

The tinkly music started to play as Mr Gideon climbed into the driver's seat and pulled away from the kerb. I recognised the tune – it was 'Who's Afraid of the Big Bad Wolf?' – a song which I'd always thought was strange because it sounded jolly but was actually about getting eaten, which wasn't really a happy thought. The music grew quieter as the van drove off down the road.

There was change from the ice creams, which Mum said I could keep in case we needed supplies for our Discovery invention. When I put the coins in the pocket of my school trousers, I noticed there was something already inside. It was a folded-up piece of paper.

I opened it and read it, thinking it must be a list I'd made and forgotten about. I got quite a shock. You'll understand why if you turn to Exhibit D.

> # BEWARE!
> ## DANGER LURKS AROUND
> ## EVERY CORNER!
> ## PEOPLE ARE LYING TO YOU!
> ## FRIENDS CAN BE ENEMIES!
> ## IF YOU DON'T WANT TO END UP
> ## IN THE JUNKYARD,
> ## TRUST NOBODY!!!

My first question was: how did the note get in my pocket? My second question was: who would use so many exclamation marks in such an alarming way? My third question was: what the heck was The Junkyard? My fourth was: what was the crazy note on about?

Lottie

Lorelai came over before we'd even finished our ice creams, so Sadie and I sat in our room, watching TV to keep out of her way. And then Mo thumped in.

'What have you done with Schrodinger?' he shouted.

'Chill out, Mo. I haven't done anything with Tiger,' I said.

'She has, then,' he pointed at Sadie.

'Eow,' Sadie shook her head.

'What's happened to him?' I said.

'He always waits on my bed for me to come home from school. He wasn't there when I got back and I can't find him anywhere.'

Sadie and I looked at each other. We really liked that fat, ginger cat.

'We'll help you look.'

We searched the house but there was no sign of him.

'He must have gone out and not come back,' Mo said, trying not to cry.

'Do you think he got lost?' I asked.

'He's lived on this road all of his life – he knows it really well. I don't think he could have got lost.'

'Prewow,' Sadie said, stroking Mo's arm.

'Do you think maybe he got homesick for your old house?' I said.

Mo sniffed. 'That's possible, I suppose. He could have gone there.'

'It's only over the road – we could go and take a peek.'

'I don't want to ask Mum while that lady is here.'

'Exactly: Lorelai is here, so we don't even have to ask her permission. And we'll be home with Schrody before Emma even notices.'

'Well, there is a back way we could go so nobody would see us from the street...' Mo said.

'I like the way you're thinking, partner,' I said. 'Sadie, would you please stay here to provide distraction and cover, if necessary?'

Sadie saluted.

I turned to Mo and smiled. 'Let's go.'

Searching for Schrodinger

Lottie

We snuck out of the front door as quietly as possible. I was born with the grace of a ballerina and the cunning of a fox, so I always excel in that type of situation. Mo was a bit more noticeable, with his hair and his clumsiness, but at least he was very short.

We crossed the road, but instead of walking up to Lorelai's front door, Mo turned right. We ran up the street until we came to a quiet side-road called Mayland Drive. Halfway down Mayland, there was an alley, wide enough for a car to pass through. I realised it led us behind the houses on our road, and towards their gardens.

'This is the one,' Mo said. 'I bet Schrodinger is here.'

We were standing by a fence that was taller than my dad. It was solid, so we couldn't see through, and the gate was locked.

'How are we going to get in?' I asked, pointing at the enormous padlock.

'Right here,' Mo said, pulling at some planks at the bottom of the fence. The planks moved enough to make a small hole, just the right size for me to crawl – and for Mo to squeeze himself – through.

It suddenly felt rather adventury and exciting.

The garden was small: just a lawn and a patio, with no trees and nowhere to hide.

'We'd better be quick,' I said. 'If Lorelai comes back and looks out of the window, she'll see us immediately.'

'He's not here.' Mo looked around. 'I wonder if he's gone into the house?'

'She's probably got him in there doing the washing up and sewing her clothes with all the local squirrels and blue tits.'

'What?'

'You know, like a Disney princess?'

'But cats can't do the washing-up, Lottie. They don't like water.'

'Just forget it, Mo.' For a clever boy, he really was clueless sometimes. 'How can we look inside if all the curtains are closed?'

'Cat flap,' Mo pointed at the back door.

We knelt down on the paving stones, getting

dirt and dust all over our uniforms. Mo pushed open the flap and stuck his head in.

'That's weird,' he said.

'Are there foxes doing the hoovering? Let me see!'

'No, it's a mess. Didn't she say she'd decorated and that?'

'She did. And bought new furniture.'

'It still has the exact same stuff in it that it did when I lived there. Nothing's different.'

'Why would she lie? And why does she really keep the curtains closed all the time?'

'Maybe to hide the mess. You should see it, Lottie, there are boxes and piles of stuff everywhere.'

'Let me have a look!'

'Fine, but hurry up.' Mo shuffled back to make way for me.

Mo was right – the place was a dump. There were empty food packets overflowing from the bin – mostly cakes and sweets. Every surface was covered with what looked like electrical parts: wires, microchips and circuit boards. In one corner there was what looked like a shiny new TV, which for some reason had been taken apart and was in pieces on the floor.

'This is all very strange,' I said. 'What is she up to?'

I shuffled back. 'Call Schrody and let's get out of here.'

Mo pushed his face through the flap again.

'I can see him in the hallway!' he bounced up and down, banging his head. 'Schrodinger!' he called, 'Come here Schro!' He made kissy noises.

'We should have brought some ham,' I said. Schrody loves ham.

'He's not allowed to eat ham,' said Mo. 'The vet told us. You haven't been giving him ham, have you?'

'No, of course not.' It didn't seem like a good time to tell Mo that Sadie and I had been using ham in our attempts to train Schrodinger to do back flips.

'Schrodinger! That's it, come on!'

Mo pushed himself further in.

'I've almost got him,' he said.

There was a moment of silence, and then Mo whispered, 'Lottie, nobody's supposed to live here except Laura, right?'

'It's *Lorelai*, Mo. It really isn't that difficult. And don't worry – she definitely said she lives alone. Many, many times.'

'Someone's here. Two people, maybe. I can hear voices upstairs.'

'Grab Schrody and get out, now!'

'Oh, bums, I think they're coming down the stairs.'

'Have you got him yet?'

'Yes!' He started wriggling his bottom. 'I'm coming out.'

He started sliding his knees back and I turned to run.

'Lottie!' he said. 'I'm stuck!'

'No, Mo, you simply cannot be stuck!'

'I'm stuck and they're coming down the stairs. Oh my god. What am I going to do? They're going to catch me!' He started kicking his feet up and down.

'First, don't panic. Second, think yourself small.'

'What do you mean?' Mo wailed.

'Imagine that you're a teeny tiny hedgehog. I'm going to pull you from your waist,' I said.

'Won't you get prickled?' he said, sounding even more panicked.

'JUST THINK SMALL!' I said, and I pulled him as hard as I could.

'They're getting closer,' he yelped. 'Pull harder!'

I pulled and pulled, and it felt like he wasn't budging at all. He is rather round, after all. But suddenly he sort of popped out, with Schrodinger in his arms, and we both fell back in a heap.

As we lay there, red and out of breath, we heard loud voices. Whoever had been walking down the stairs had obviously come into the kitchen. We stayed low, but moved our ears closer to the cat flap so we could hear what they were saying. It made no sense for anyone to be there.

'Will you make me some food before you go out again? I'm hungry!' a whiny voice said – it sounded like a kid.

'Get it yourself,' a very low, rough voice answered. 'If it wasn't for you, I wouldn't have to be out collecting parts every night.'

'I said I'm sorry. I'm trying to sort it out. There's no need to starve me.'

I heard a door slam.

'My two favourite boys aren't fighting again, are they?' Lorelai was home.

'No,' the other voices said at the same time.

'Did you find out anything new from over the road?' the man said.

'Had to make up some excuses to the brats,' she said. (How dare she?)

'Did they buy it?'

'Well, of course they did, I'm sweet as syrup. Their idiot of a mother thinks I'm her new best friend.'

I held tightly on to Mo's arm to stop him from trying to break the door down in a rage.

'Don't fret, my loves,' Lorelai carried on. 'We have lots of time to make a decision while we build the replacement cuff. For now, we keep eyes on them at all times. Understood?'

'Yeah,' they answered.

'And whether it's the stout, red-headed, bumbling boy, or that precocious princess girl with the ridiculous hairstyles, we'll look forward to the day when we get rid of one of them for good.'

Lore-liar

Lottie:
So – plot twist! Lorelai isn't Rapunzel after all, she's actually Mother Gothel, which totally explains her granny neck.

Mo:
Why do you have to make everything weird?

Lottie:
Why do you have to make everything boring? You know when you're really sick, and afterwards your mum makes you eat dry toast with nothing on it? That's what you are, Mo. You are dry toast.

Mo:
That's hardly even an insult. I get called worse things every day at school.

Lottie:
The point is that we were involved in a real-life murder mystery – even you have to admit it was exciting.

Mo:

There was NO murder – stop exaggerating, Lottie. And if by exciting, you mean terrifying, then yes, it was.

Lottie:

We knew two things for sure: that Lorelai wanted to get rid of us; that she had at least two people helping her; and that we were in it together.

Mo:

That's three things. We knew three things for sure.

Lottie:

What we didn't know was why she hated us, or who she was working with…

Mo:

So we ran home as fast as we could and shut ourselves in my room to talk about it.

Lottie:

I'd like to point out that we shut ourselves in Mo's room because his room was the biggest. Of course, Mo had to have the biggest room, because he's hashtag-sensitive. Totally unfair.

Mo:

It's also completely irrelevant. And stop hashtagging things. It's so annoying.

Lottie:

Hashtag-you, hashtag-are, hashtag-annoying, hashtag-Mo.

Mo tries and fails to push Lottie off her chair, so she pushes Mo off his. There is a loud thud as his bottom hits the floor

Mo

'Why would Lorelai want to get rid of us?' Lottie asked. 'I mean, I can understand why she'd want to get rid of you, but not me – I'm adorable! Maybe she meant Sadie.'

'But she said the thing about the ridiculous hairstyles. That's definitely you.'

'My hairstyles are awesome, though.' She thought for a moment. 'Unless she's jealous. That must be it! And, in that case, I can understand why she'd want to get rid of me, but not you.'

Nothing Lottie said made sense. 'So, do you want her to want to get rid of you?'

'Yes. I don't see why you should be the special one she wants to get rid of.' Lottie threw herself on my bed WITH HER SHOES ON and buried her face in my pillow.

'The scary, crazy lady didn't say just me, though, she said both of us, remember?'

'Oh yes, she did. Thanks, Mo, you're actually quite sweet sometimes.'

'Right. So now we've established that both of our lives are in danger, and that you're happy about it…?'

She smiled and nodded.

'…We need to work out what we've done, and who those other people in the house were.'

'And also,' Lottie said, 'what was she saying about choosing one of us? Why only one of us? Why not both?'

'You want her to choose you, don't you?'

'I'll be highly offended if she chooses you, if that's what you mean.'

Absolutely mental. 'I'll tell you what, if she does choose me to be kidnapped or killed, I'll tell her to take you instead.'

'You'd do that for me?' Lottie's face lit up.

'Sure,' I said.

She hugged me. The only people who had ever hugged me were my mum and my nan. I felt my cheeks get hot.

'I have to show you something,' I said, and I took the note I'd found in my pocket out of my secret box.

Lottie gasped. 'I have one, too!' She unfolded a piece of paper and put it on the floor in front of us.

'They've obviously come from the same person,' I said. 'But who?'

'And are they really trying to help us, or is it all a trick?'

'We should make a list of suspects,' I said.

'That's a great idea, Mo! We can write down everything we know about anyone who's been acting suspiciously, starting with the Wicked Witch of the Road.'

'OK, so we'll put down Lori-thingy... Mr Gideon's a bit creepy.'

'Yes, but I don't see how anyone who makes ice cream that tastes like heaven could be trying to hurt us,' said Lottie.

'I know, but his arm is weird.'

'You're putting him on our hit list because his arm is weird?'

'Yes.'

'Fine. Mr Gideon, the bringer of joy, can go on the list. That disgraceful excuse for a lollipop man should go on it, too.'

'I kind of feel sorry for him, though,' I said.

'Because he's a loser?' Lottie rolled her eyes.

'No.'

'Because he's almost killed half the kids at school?'

'No.'

'Why then?'

'I'm not sure, I just... I don't know. I like his face.'

'Don't forget he has freaky, bulging pocket, full of mouse brains,' Lottie said.

'OK, OK, we'll put him on the list.'

We wrote the names in my scrapbook. If you want to see the list we made, please look at Exhibit G.

Lorelai
Mr Gideon
Hector (lollipop man)

'There's someone else I think we should put in,' Lottie said, giving me a sneaky side-eye.

'Who?'

'Jax.'

'Why?' I knew it was just because she didn't like him.

'First,' Lottie said, as though she'd prepared her answers, 'he's new. We don't really know him.'

'You're new,' I said.

'Second,' Lottie completely ignored me, 'There was a kid at Lorelai's house. It sounded like him.'

'We couldn't hear properly through the door – not enough to tell who it was. And I've never heard Jax talk in that whiny voice.'

'Third,' she carried on. 'Do you not find it strange how he agrees with everything you say?'

'No,' I said. 'Why would that be strange? I'm right pretty much all of the time.'

'Fourth, he was acting like a lunatic with the lost property.'

'He's excited about the competition. He was being enthusiastic.'

'And fifth,' she pushed a photo towards me, 'Look at this.'

'It's an old school photo, so what?' I said.

'Look at this boy here, Mo,' she said, stabbing at a kid in the front row with her finger. 'Tell me that isn't Jax's identical twin.'

It did look like Jax, but what was she getting at? The picture was from ten years ago. It had nothing to do with him.

'So, that kid looks like Jax,' I shrugged.

'That kid looks exactly the same as Jax,' Lottie said. 'If it wasn't impossible, I'd even say it was Jax.'

'But it is impossible!' She was making me so mad. 'Just because you can't handle the fact that Jax wants to be my friend and not yours, doesn't mean he's some evil psycho, who apparently time travels just so he can be in Year 6 at St Pippins for ever.'

'I knew you'd react like this,' she rolled her eyes. 'Sometimes you're so unreasonable, Mo.'

'And I thought you were actually being nice, helping me find Schrodinger, but you're as annoying as ever.'

She got up and stormed out of my room. 'We need a timeout!' she yelled, and slammed the door.

Fine with me.

Keeping an Eye on Jax

Lottie

We hardly spoke to each other for the rest of the day. Mo was the most stubborn person I've ever met and I couldn't get him to see Jax as anything other than Mr Awesome. It was infuriating.

I constantly looked over at Lorelai's house, but didn't see her at all. The curtains were always closed, the lights went on in every room as soon as it got dark and from what I could tell, they stayed on all night. What on earth could she be doing in there? And did it have something to do with all those electrical parts?

By the next morning, Mo and I had both calmed down enough to talk to each other on the way to school. I decided not to mention Jax again. Instead, I'd keep an eye on him and see if I could trick him into giving himself away. I wasn't a hundred per cent sure I was right about him – my head said he couldn't possibly be the boy from the photo, but my heart was telling me that he didn't add up.

'Did you come up with any reasons why someone might want to get rid of you?' Mo asked as we reached the crossing.

'Other than jealousy, of course not,' I said. 'You know me, Mo, I'm spectacular. What about you?'

'I'm not sure,' Mo said. 'Lots of people think I'm weird and don't really like me.'

I looked across at him as he bent down to pick up a homework diary that someone had dropped onto the floor. If anyone else had said that about not being liked, they probably would have been a big fat attention-seeker. But not Mo.

'This is Priya's from Year 4,' his face lit up. 'I'll find her in the playground and give it back.'

Yes, he could be maddening, but he was also one of the sweetest people in the world. I'd never known anyone quite like him, and being original is always a good thing.

We were given more time in class to work on our Discovery Day Competition entry, so we spent half the morning in that awful, dusty cupboard.

'We're not making any progress at all,' I said, sitting in the corner.

Jax carried on throwing stuff around, while Mo watched him with a frown on his face.

'Lottie's right,' Mo said. (I know: shocker!) 'We can't get the testing equipment or chemicals, so all we have is a database. We're not going to get any of these items back to their owners.'

'And we're not going to win a competition with a boring database.'

'Maybe we should brainstorm again?' Mo looked up at Jax, as though he wanted his permission.

'Yeah, let's just give this idea one more try first, though,' Jax said.

'But we're running out of time,' Mo said.

'We've got plenty of time left,' Jax said. 'Anyway, what did you guys get up to last night?'

'Not much,' I said.

'That's not true, Lottie. Schrodinger got lost, remember?' Mo nudged me.

'Who's Schrodinger?' Jax asked.

'Just our cat,' I said.

'Your cat's called Schrodinger?' Jax looked around for a moment. 'So when he was lost, he was both alive and dead until you found him? Cool.'

Mo and Jax were falling over laughing.

I didn't get it. Some kind of bizarre science joke, I suppose.

'But that's not really possible, is it?' I said. 'To

be two things at once, or in two places at the same time, or even in one place at two times?'

Jax's face darkened, suddenly. It was like storm clouds covering up the sun.

'If you're talking about time travel, Lottie,' Mo said, really not picking up on the vibe, 'it actually is possible, in theory.'

'But nobody's worked out how to do it yet. Right?' Jax said.

'Right,' Mo agreed, 'but I'm sure somebody will in the future.'

'So, did you find him?' Jax said, as if he was trying to change the subject.

I tried to give Mo a subtle shake of the head. I thought we were better off keeping to ourselves what happened, especially as Jax was acting more suspiciously by the second.

But Mo was as clueless as ever. 'Yes, he'd gone back to my old house across the road.'

'Wait – your old house is across the road from your new house?' Jax said.

'Exactly opposite,' Mo nodded. 'A lady lives there now; she… Ow!'

That's right; I had kicked Mo in the leg to shut him up.

'Schrodinger was sitting outside the front of the house and came running when we called him,' I said. 'We didn't even have to go down the front steps.'

I ignored Mo's funny look.

Jax carried on pulling boxes from the top shelf. 'You know,' he said, 'I really love cats and Schrodinger sounds amazing. I'd like to meet him one day.'

Mo's eyes widened with excitement, and before I could stop him, he'd said, 'You could come over after school, if you like? I know Mum won't mind.'

'Are you sure? I wouldn't want to inconvenience your family?'

'My mum is the nicest – she won't mind at all,' Mo said, smiling his face off.

'OK, cool, I'll come today, then. Thanks, mate.'

I've never seen Mo as happy as he looked when we left school with shady Jax. He was completely taken in by him – I didn't know how I was going to get him to see that Jax was most definitely up to something.

'Oh, look, Mr Gideon is parked right outside the school,' Mo said. 'Let's get ice creams.'

'We should definitely do that,' I said, speeding up so we could make it to the van before anyone else.

'I don't really feel like ice cream,' Jax said.

'What?' Mo looked at him like he was mad.

'I'd rather get back to your house.'

'I don't understand,' Mo said. 'You don't want ice cream?'

'Nah,' Jax said, putting his hands in his pockets.

'But this is Mr Gideon's ice cream,' I said. 'It's special.'

We were close to the van now, and I could see Mr Gideon leaning out of the hatch, looking up and down the street. He seemed to spot us. He looked from me, to Mo, to Jax, hesitated, and then disappeared back inside his van.

'He's not leaving, is he?' Mo was in a panic.

'Why would he leave?' I asked. 'We haven't got our ice creams yet!' I started running towards the van at the same time as Hector the lollipop man, who was waving his stick around.

'No parking on the zig-zags!' he yelled. 'No ice cream vans within one hundred and fifty metres of the school! It's the law! You're breaking the law!'

He had longer legs than me and Mo, and it was obvious he was going to get to Mr Gideon before we did. I heard the engine start, and Mr Gideon's van started moving off.

'And don't come back!' Hector shouted, whacking the back of the van with his stick. The top part snapped off and flew into a tree at the side of the road. While he ran after it, Mo and I finally got to the empty spot where the van had been. I don't know why, but it felt so dreadfully awful that Mr Gideon had gone. My eyes filled with tears and I really thought I was going to cry.

Mo threw his bag on the floor in a huff and then crouched beside it, covering his eyes with his hands.

'Er, guys,' Jax said. 'It's just ice cream.'

'How dare you?' I turned on him. 'You don't. Even. Know.'

'I'm sure he'll be around again later.'

'You think?' Mo looked up.

'Yeah, definitely. This is his patch – he's not going to give up, it would be bad for business.'

Mo started picking up the things that had fallen out of his bag. 'This isn't mine,' he said, looking at a large envelope that was lying on the ground right where Mr Gideon had been. 'I'd better take it and try to work out who it belongs to.'

'Maybe it's Mr Gideon's,' I said. 'We should probably try to find him.'

'Nah,' said Jax, and he started walking in the direction of our house.

'How do you know which way to go?' I asked him.

'Mo must have told me,' he said.

'Did you, Mo?' I asked.

'If we run, we might be able to catch Mr Gideon up,' Mo said, gazing into the distance.

Ice Cream Panic

Mo

We were halfway up Fairfield Road (you can see our route on Exhibit F, which is a map) when I heard a tinkly tune playing quietly in the distance. I turned to see Mr Gideon's ice cream van crawling up the road behind us.

'There he is!' Lottie said.

'Do you have any money? I'll pay you back?' I said.

'My money's at home!' she wailed, throwing half the contents of her bag out onto the pavement and feeling around in the corners anyway.

'Do you have any money, Jax?' I said.

'No. We should just go.'

Mr Gideon's van stopped about twenty metres away, the ice cream man staring ahead with the engine still running. A couple of kids knocked eagerly on the side.

'They're going to get all the ice cream!' I said, feeling devastated.

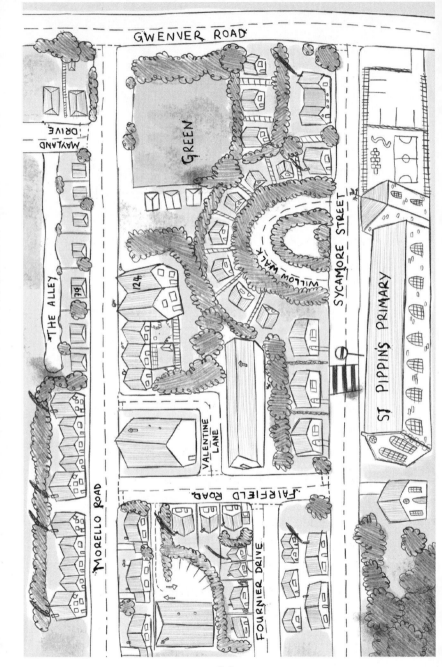

'Let's run home and get our money boxes.' Lottie jumped over her belongings that were in a heap on the ground, and broke into a jog.

'What about your stuff, though?' I said.

'It doesn't matter – just leave it!'

It went against everything I believed in, but I needed ice cream, so I turned away and we started to run, thinking we'd get home in time to get some cash and make it back to the van. The sound of the engine grew louder. I looked over my shoulder to see the van behind us again.

'Take the shortcut!' I said, veering off down a side-road with Lottie while Jax trailed behind. There were no front doors on the road we were cutting down, so Mr Gideon would definitely go the long way around.

But the jangly music got closer again, and I could see the ice cream van turning into the road we were racing down. It was almost as if it was following us.

'We'll never make it!' Lottie yelled, as we flew onto our street.

'We have to make it!' I yelled back.

'I have cramp – you go ahead,' Jax said, stopping to sit on a garden wall.

We made it to Morello Road, ran up the steps to our house and tore into the kitchen.

'Goodness!' Mum said. 'Were you racing?'

'Money,' I panted. 'Ice cream.'

'Quick,' Lottie wheezed.

'Please,' I added.

'OK, but you'd better eat your dinner,' Mum said, handing us money out of her purse.

'You're the best, Mum!' I shouted, as we ran back out of the door, with Sadie right behind us.

Mr Gideon was parked right outside our house.

'Hello, Mr Gideon,' I said, still out of breath. 'Vanilla cone, please. Two flakes. Strawberry sauce.'

As Mr Gideon turned, I saw a small movement over the road at my old house. The curtains were all closed again, but one of them was moving, as though somebody had just been peeping through a gap. It kind of gave me the creeps.

Mr Gideon thrust the cone at me with a grunt and turned to Lottie.

'I'll have the same as him, please,' she said.

'You can't have the same as me,' I said, feeling very annoyed.

'Why not?'

'Because that's what I have.'

'So you own the top secret recipe of a vanilla cone with two flakes and strawberry sauce, do you?'

I gave her a dirty look and licked a drip of sauce that was dribbling down my cone.

'Meowl,' Sadie said.

'Sadie will have the same, too, please, Mr Gideon.'

I huffed.

As Mr Gideon turned with the two cones in his hand, a drop of sweat flicked off his forehead and landed on one of them.

'Yuck,' I said.

'Erm, Mr Gideon,' Lottie said, 'Would you mind exchanging this one, please? I don't think it meets health and safety requirements.'

She took the non-sweaty cone and gave it to Sadie, waiting for Mr Gideon to make her another one. There was an awkward moment when everyone was perfectly still: Sadie and me with our cones, Lottie looking hopefully up at the hatch, and Mr Gideon still holding out the contaminated ice cream with that weird patchwork arm of his. Then he put his left hand out for the money.

'Oh, right,' Lottie said quietly.

I almost felt sorry for her.

She gave him the money and took the ice cream, which was starting to melt. Mr Gideon drove off.

'I'm still eating it,' she said. 'Don't judge me.'

I should have taken the opportunity to insult her over it, but I actually couldn't blame her. The ice cream was so damn good. I would have eaten it if it had been dropped on the floor.

Mum seemed really happy when I brought Jax home. She tried to be cool about it, but I could tell she was relieved that I finally had a friend. She fussed about, asking Jax what snacks he liked and giving us a massive tray of biscuits to eat up in my room.

Lottie and me had been getting on better since the Schrodinger incident, but she was still being a bit rude to Jax. I didn't mind that much, because Jax was apparently the only person at school who liked me more than her, but it made working on the Discovery Competition difficult.

We sat on my bedroom floor with some pens and paper, eating Jammie Dodgers.

'So if your dad is with Mo's mum,' Jax said to Lottie, 'what happened to your mum?'

'She's leading an expedition in the South American rainforest, actually. She's looking for a rare flower which contains an ingredient that can cure leprosy.'

It was a bit strange, because I was sure she'd said her mum was digging up a fossil.

'She'll come back for Sadie and me once she's finished her work. She's very important, you know.'

I was about to say something, but I stopped myself. I always found it difficult to tell people about my dad, so maybe Lottie felt the same way about her mum. If she wanted to make things up to avoid telling people the truth, it was her business. As much as I liked Jax, I didn't want to embarrass Lottie in front of him.

I held my breath, thinking Jax was going to ask me what happened to my dad. It was the obvious question to ask, seeing as he was so interested in our family situation. But instead he started looking around my room.

'So where's your collection, then, Mo?' he said. 'You know, all the junk you've found.'

'Mostly in the garage,' I said.

'Oh,' Jax said, frowning. Probably he realised how hard it was for me to be separated from my collection.

'There's, like, a million boxes of the stuff,' said Lottie. 'He's only allowed to keep one box of it in the house.'

'And where's that?' he stood up, as though he was going to start ransacking my room like he did with the lost property.

'It's away,' I said. I didn't want to be mean, but my box was private and the thought of Jax rummaging through my things made me feel very anxious.

'It's a secret box,' Lottie explained. 'We all have one. Nobody is allowed to look in them.'

'So, what's in your box, then?' Jax raised an eyebrow.

'A magical golden egg,' Lottie said. 'I won it in a battle of wits against a sword swallower from Tibet.'

'If you don't want to tell me, you should just say so,' Jax said.

'I just did tell you,' Lottie said.

'Shall we write down some new ideas for the

competition?' I pulled the paper towards me and took the lid off a pen.

'Finally,' Lottie said. 'I think we're all agreed that the forensic lost-property testing hasn't been a success.'

'It was a good idea, though,' I said.

'It was a great idea, but not practical, and also not that invention-y.' Lottie bit her lip. 'We need something new and exciting. We need the wow factor. We need to kill it. We need to blow everyone's minds. We need something hashtaggable...'

'You guys really want to win, don't you?' Jax said.

'Yes!' we answered at the same time.

'The thing with the lost property,' Lottie said, 'is that some of it is so old, the people who lost it probably don't even remember it existed. It's like, if I lost a sock, I'd probably be annoyed about it for a day, and then I'd forget about it and get some new ones.'

'But losing stuff is awful,' I said. 'Sometimes, when you lose something, there's just a hole in your life that you can never fill.'

Jax and Lottie both looked at me.

'That's true sometimes, Mo,' said Lottie. 'But most of the time when things go missing, people move on. What would be better than trying to get a bunch of junk back to its owners, is inventing a way to stop you from losing the things that really are important to you.'

'I don't know,' said Jax. 'Sounds a bit lame.'

'Actually, I think that's quite a good idea.' Perhaps I'd been looking at it the wrong way. Imagine if I could invent something that could stop my most important things from ever getting lost again. 'Like Schrodinger,' I said.

'Exactly!' Lottie jumped up. 'Schrodinger can't be replaced. Let's think up something that means we can always get him back if he runs off.'

'I'm not saying no,' Jax said. 'But can we just go over some other ideas, first?'

'But this is a great idea!' Lottie said.

'We're supposed to be working in a team,' said Jax.

'He's right, Lottie, we are,' I said.

'Fine. You two go over a load of pointless, boring ideas. I'm going to get started on an invention to stop Schrody from getting lost again.'

She did this dramatic, exaggerated walk out of

the room and kind of angrily pranced down the stairs.

'Not much of a team player, is she?' Jax said. 'Not like you, Mo.' He walked over to the window. 'So which house did you used to live in?'

'That one,' I pointed, 'With the crumbly wall at the front and the sky-blue door. A lady called Laura, or Laurel, or something, lives there now.'

'How long did you live there?'

'All my life, until a few weeks ago.' I looked over at the covered windows. 'I miss that house.'

'Who lived there before you?'

'I don't know. My mum moved in when she was pregnant with me. You could ask her? She might know.'

I saw Jax give me a side-eye.

'So you don't know what was there when your mum moved in? She never mentioned anything?'

It seemed like a weird question. For the first time, I wondered if Lottie was right to be suspicious of him.

'We should get back to work,' I said. 'Then we'll go downstairs in a bit and see how Lottie's getting on.'

A New Invention

Lottie

'Come on, Sadie, help me think of an invention.'

Sadie was in the living room watching cartoons, so I flung myself down on the sofa next to her. I was annoyed with Jax, and annoyed with Mo for not seeing how annoying Jax was. I didn't want them to beat me. I had to think up the best invention ever.

Sadie giggled at the TV, as the coyote tried to catch the roadrunner using some metal boots and a giant magnet. He ended up getting a kick in the boy bits and a magnet to the head. But it gave me an idea.

'Sadie, I need your assistance in the kitchen!'

'Merrrrrrow,' said Sadie, following me out of the door.

Emma was a bit worried when she heard our idea, but she's such a pushover, I soon got her to get out some ingredients and leave us to it.

I should probably tell you that I am an excellent baker. I prefer creating by myself to following a recipe, though. Recipes are for people who have no imagination.

And there would definitely be no recipe for what I had in mind.

Sadie and I worked tirelessly for a whole thirty minutes, creating something so new and exciting that people were going to pee their pants when they saw them.

'Do you need any help, girls?' Emma peered around the corner.

'No, no, we have everything under control,' I said while Sadie pushed her out of the room with floury hands.

'Perow mew?' Sadie said.

'Yes, Sadie, definitely more glitter. All the colours.'

Edible glitter was one of our favourite ingredients. We tried to incorporate it into most of our bakes, usually for decorative purposes. But this time the glitter was functional as well as beautiful. It was the most important part of our creation.

Mo and Jax came into the kitchen just as we were taking them out of the oven.

'What are they?' Mo said, peering at them.

'They smell quite nice.'

'Of course they smell nice,' I said, sprinkling the leftover glitter into my fishtail braid so that, firstly, I would look like a mermaid and, secondly, I would match my invention.

'They look… interesting,' said Jax, sneering at them. 'What exactly are they?'

'They're our invention for the Discovery Competition,' I said.

'And how exactly are little biscuit balls an invention?' Jax said, poking one.

'For your information, they're called Glitter Balls (™). And they are not only delicious, but also the perfect way to bring your missing pets back to you.'

'How do they work?' Mo said.

'I'm glad you asked, Mo. Allow me to demonstrate, with the help of my awesome assistant, Sadie.'

Sadie put a Glitter Ball (™) into her mouth, chewed and swallowed.

'You feed them to your sister?' Jax said, rolling his eyes.

Sadie swallowed and gave me a thumbs-up. 'Merow.'

'What was that?' Jax sneered. 'Can't she talk properly?'

'She talks all the time!' Jax was really annoying me. 'Doesn't she, Mo?'

'Well, yes.' Mo looked uncomfortable. 'But Jax probably didn't realise she was talking because she has her own, you know, special language.'

'Do you mean that squeaking?' Jax said.

'Hssssssssss,' said Sadie.

'So, what happens now?' Mo asked. 'With the Glitter Ball (™) I mean?'

'Sadie will now leave the room and, using this large magnet, I will pull her back into the kitchen.'

'Really?' Mo said. 'How will that work?'

'Inside the crunchy crust of the Glitter Balls (™), there is a surprise liquid centre filled with glitter. Glitter is metal. Magnets suck metal towards them. Simple.'

Jax snorted. 'Go on, then, give it a try.'

I lifted the magnet and pointed it towards the open door.

Nothing happened.

'Maybe the magnet is too small,' I said. 'I'll go a bit nearer.'

Still no sign of Sadie.

'I can't believe it didn't work!' I said, feeling ever so disappointed. 'You might as well come back, Sadie,' I called out of the door.

'I think, maybe, there isn't enough metal,' Mo said.

'More glitter?' I said. Sadie grabbed five more Glitter Balls (™) and started cramming them into her mouth.

'I'm sorry, Lottie, I still don't think it will be enough,' Mo said. 'It was a brilliant idea, though.'

'Yeah, genius,' Jax sniggered.

I picked up the tray and carried it over to the bin. All that hard work wasted.

'Don't throw them away – maybe they'll be useful for something else,' Mo said. 'May I try one? They look yummy.'

'Sure,' I said. 'Do you think at least that they might make your poo sparkly?'

'That's a definite possibility,' Mo said. 'I'll have one and report back to you later.'

'Thanks, Mo.' I smiled and realised I was actually getting quite fond of him.

'Oh, blimey,' Emma said, walking into the kitchen and looking at the mess. 'Are you finished, girls? I need to get the dinner on.'

'Yes, we're finished,' I said. 'Could I please have a tub to store my Glitter Balls (™) in?'

'Sure, I'll get one. They look amazing,' Emma rummaged around in a cupboard as Dad walked through the door.

'What have you made this time, girls?' he said, looking around the kitchen. 'I hope you're planning to clean up this mess and not leave it for Emma.'

'Actually, we're quite tired from all our hard work,' I said. 'We might need a sit down.'

'Meooooooooow,' Sadie yawned.

'Lottie, Sadie: get your butts over to the sink and start washing up. Right now.' Dad was obviously cross.

'It's OK, Spencer! Look: the kids have a friend over,' Emma nudged Dad and nodded at Jax. 'This is Jax.'

'Oh, right,' Dad said. 'Hi there, Jax.'

'What are your plans for dinner, sweetheart?' said Emma.

'Oh, I guess I'd better go home.'

'You can eat with us, if you like and if your parents don't mind,' Emma said.

'My parents don't really do much cooking,' Jax said, 'So I'm sure it would be OK with them.'

'Lovely.' Emma smiled at Dad. 'Why don't you kids go and watch some TV, and I'll call you when it's ready.'

'Mrow,' Sadie said, looking right at Jax.

'Sadie, you shouldn't really use that kind of language,' Emma tried her best to look strict.

'So even you can understand her now?' Mo was annoyed.

'Well, you know, Sadie and I spend a lot of time together while you two are at school,' Emma said. 'It really isn't difficult, once you get used to it.'

Mo muttered to himself as we walked into the living room.

'I'm just going to use the bathroom,' Jax said, and he disappeared upstairs.

'Jax has been acting a bit weird,' Mo whispered to me as soon as he was gone.

'Oh, really – do you think?' I said, rolling my eyes.

'Yes, he's so set on doing the old idea for the Discovery Competition, when it obviously isn't going to work. And he was asking some strange questions.' He completely missed my sarcasm, as always.

'Let's wait until he's gone and then discuss it in

your room,' I said, excited at the thought of doing some secret bad-mouthing. 'In the meantime, keep a close eye on him.'

I watched Jax through dinner but he didn't do anything out of the ordinary – in fact, he seemed to chill out a bit and was kind of nice. He ate like he hadn't been fed in months, though. I wondered if maybe his parents didn't look after him very well. It wasn't a happy thought, and it almost made me not look forward to being mean about him as soon as he left.

He went home straight after dinner, saying his Mum was waiting for him around the corner in her car.

Mo and I stood at the window, watching him run down the road.

'Where did he say he lived?' I asked.

'He didn't.'

A movement across the street caught my eye. 'Mo, look!' I nudged him. Lorelai was standing at her downstairs window, watching Jax.

'You don't think she's after Jax, too, do you?' Mo said.

'No, I don't think so.' Clearly Mo still needed persuading that Jax was not his friend.

Lorelai turned her face, suddenly, and saw us looking over at her.

'Bum-biscuits!' Mo said, and we ducked down, out of sight.

We Finally Learn
a Few Things

Mo

Lottie sat on my bed, styling Schrodinger's hair into a silly spike while I tipped everything out of my school bag so I could repack it. It was still a mess from when I threw it on the floor after Mr Gideon drove off.

'You need to listen to me about this, Mo,' Lottie said. 'I know you think he's your friend, but he's not.'

'I agree that he acts a bit funny sometimes, but that doesn't mean he's evil.'

Lottie side-eyed me. 'You're a scientist, right, Mo? Like your dad?'

'Yes. A serious one.'

'So, a scientist looks for clues and evidence to back up his theories. He doesn't just believe something randomly and blindly without thinking it through.'

'But something's telling me that he's not a bad

113

guy. I can't explain it – it's just a feeling I have about him.'

'That's because you're too soft-hearted, Mo. You're kind to losers and weirdos. It's a classic underdog rooting for the other underdogs thing.'

'That sounded like one of those insults that's made to sound like a compliment,' I said.

'Wrong again, Mo. It was a compliment disguised as an insult.'

'You're so confusing.'

'My point is,' Lottie said, 'if there's anyone in the surrounding area who is alone, an oddball or a bit useless, you instantly like them.'

'Oh, I forgot about this,' I said, pulling the envelope I'd found earlier out of the pile.

'That is a dreadful lie, Mo Appleby,' Lottie said. 'I bet you've been itching to have a look in that envelope since we got home.'

It was true, and it made me smile, even though I didn't want to.

'OMG, did you finally find your sense of humour?' Lottie said. 'Open it then, before you explode.'

The envelope was large and fat, with no name or address on the front.

'It's sealed, though,' I said, feeling bad. 'Maybe I shouldn't.'

'Well then you'll never be able to get it back to its owner,' said Lottie. 'Just do it, Mo.'

I carefully opened the envelope, trying not to rip the paper so that I could reseal it afterwards. Inside was a thick pile of papers and on top of them was another note.

'What the bumfluff?'

Take a look at Exhibit H:

**IT IS NOT WHAT YOU HAVE DONE,
BUT WHAT YOU WILL DO
THAT HAS LED YOU TO DANGER!**
**THE CONTENTS OF THIS
ENVELOPE MAY HELP YOU.**
TRUST NOBODY

Lottie gasped and ran over to where I was sitting on the floor. 'Let me see!'

'Not what you have done, but what you will do...' I read it again, trying to make sense of it. 'But how could anybody be angry with me for something I haven't even done yet? How do they even know I'm going to do it?'

'Excuse me,' Lottie snatched the note from me. 'How do you know this was meant for you? I got the first note, remember, the mystery note-writer might have meant for me to find the envelope.'

'Give it back, Lottie. I'm the one who finds things – it was obviously left for me.'

'Maybe you were meant to find it so you could give it to me!'

'Let's just look together,' I said. 'OK?'

'OK.'

Mo suddenly jumps down from his chair and runs over to the camera. His hand moves towards the device and the sound becomes muffled

Lottie:
What are you doing, Mo? The recorder won't work properly if you put your hand over it.

Mo:
I know that, Lottie. That's why I've put my hand over it. I'm not an idiot!

Lottie:
If you need to pee, just say it. In life or death

situations, the normal rules of politeness and etiquette don't apply.

Mo:
I don't need to pee, I just… I'm not sure we should put everything from the envelope in the box.

Lottie:
Why not?

Mo *whispers*:
Because…

*From this point on, the voices are very quiet and muffled, so some of the conversation cannot be heard. Words and sentences that cannot be made out are represented by ****s. Swears are also represented by ****s*

Lottie:
Doesn't it **** the truth? **** **** to know.

Mo:
**** mostly, but first **** **** spoilers **** future.

Lottie:
**** **** find out ****.

Mo:
Also, **** bad. **** bad.

Lottie:
That's because ****.

Mo:
**** **** scare people a lot.

Lottie:
Just **** you're scared.

Mo:
**** too.

Lottie:
**** **** handle it. Agreed?

Mo:
Agreed.

Rustling can be heard as Mo removes his hand from the microphone. The sound suddenly becomes loud and clear again

Mo

Lottie and me leaned over the papers together.

The second sheet, behind the note, was a copy of the Discovery Competition poster.

'Why would this be in here?' Lottie asked.

'Maybe the thing that we will do that will lead us into danger has something to do with the competition,' I said.

'But how would anybody know that?' said Lottie.

'Remember Hector said that we had to win it when he was being weird outside school? And now this note says that something we're going to do will lead us into danger. It must be to do with the competition. But does that mean that winning will lead us into danger, or that winning will keep us out of danger?'

'I have to say,' Lottie frowned, 'I'm generally extremely open-minded about things, but this all seems completely absurd. It would only make sense if...'

'…The notes were written by someone who knows what is going to happen in the future,' I said.

'So maybe this person can see into the future, like a psychic,' said Lottie.

'Or maybe this person is actually from the future.'

We looked at each other.

'That seems rather unlikely,' Lottie said.

'But it is possible. In theory. "It" meaning time travel, obviously.'

'This is absolute madness,' Lottie said. 'It's brilliant! It's like the best thing that ever happened. Ever!'

'Even with the danger?' I said.

'Especially with the danger.'

I was glad someone was enjoying the situation. There were too many unknowns for me to think anything good could come out of it.

'So what we're saying is that someone from the future has come back in time to warn us that something we haven't done yet is going to get us into trouble,' I said.

'And that something is to do with the Discovery Competition.' Lottie was way too happy about it all.

'And that whether or not it's dangerous, we have to win the competition. That the future of the world depends on it.'

'Ooh, pressure. How wonderful!' Lottie smiled.

'But who is this person? How do we even know we can trust him or her?'

'We don't, Mo. That's half the fun. We need to work out who is sending the notes and if they're on our side.

'And we need to work out exactly who, other than Lore-thingy is out to get us.'

'For goodness' sake, Mo – it's Lor-A-Lie! There's an evil woman trying to destroy us, the least you can do is get her name right,' Lottie huffed at me. 'Maybe there are some answers in the rest of the papers.' She moved the poster to the side. 'What's on the next page?'

We turned to the next page and gasped. What we saw there changed everything.

JUNKERS: A QUICK GUIDE

The first Junkers are thought to have become active around the year 2030.

Initially, they were kidnappers-for-hire. If a person wanted to have another person 'removed', but not by their own hand, they could employ Junkers to do the job for them. For a price, Junkers will snatch any individual and send them to a place called 'The Junkyard', the whereabouts of which is unknown to anyone but Junkers. Once someone has been taken to The Junkyard, they never return.

In order to increase their wealth, the Junkers saw an additional use for the people they 'removed', namely, the sale of 'parts'. (This is discussed in more detail on page 2.)

In 2032, the government passed the One Child legislation – a law that aimed to control the problem of over-population. It meant that couples were restricted to having only one child, with severe penalties for those who broke the law. As a result of this, some people wanted the option to get rid of an unruly, sick or troublesome son or daughter so that they could replace it with another.

The government outlawed such practices, so the Junkers offered a removal service to those who could afford it.

Junkers have the facility to time jump (illegally).

1

PARTS

(WARNING: CONTAINS DETAILS THAT SOME MAY FIND DISTRESSING)

A large proportion of the Junkers' wealth has been accrued through the sale of 'parts'.

Rather than ending the lives of the people they junk, the Junkers keep them alive and in relative good health to provide a crop of body parts that the Junkers can harvest and sell.

People with failing or injured body parts can pay the Junkers to provide them with a replacement which, due to rapid developments in medicine during the 21st century, can be attached or inserted for an additional cost.

Because Junking involves great physical danger, Junkers themselves often need replacement parts. While unfortunate, this does allow for easier identification of some Junkers. Their body parts may appear to be mismatched. Some Junkers even keep a store of parts available, so that they can regularly change their appearance in order to conceal their identity.

It is not known what happens to the Junkers' victims once their parts have been removed, as nobody has ever returned from The Junkyard to provide an account. However, it is believed that, without proper medical care, once the victims' parts have been removed they are likely to be left to perish.

2

HOW TO SPOT A JUNKER AND WHAT TO DO IF YOU ENCOUNTER ONE

The first and most obvious mark of a Junker is that discussed on page 2, subheading: PARTS. Other signs to look out for include:

High sugar consumption – due to sugar being made illegal in 2029, a Junker who has time-jumped to the past is likely to hoard and consume many sugar-filled products, including cakes, sweets, chocolate and biscuits.

The use of an illegal addictive substance called Kandy – Junkers hide Kandy in food and use it to lure their intended victims.

A hostile attitude – if they are going to junk you, they probably don't like you.

An over-friendly attitude – if they are going to junk you, they may befriend you so they can manipulate you.

What to do if you encounter Junkers:
- Do not eat their food
- Never be alone with them
- Equip yourself with a defensive weapon, preferably one made of metal
- RUN!

On the next page you will find a safety poster containing an easily memorable poem to help your children recall these rules.

3

JUNKERS

Jumbled face and body parts, they're masters of disguise;

Unhealthy sugar cravings for biscuits, cakes and pies;

Never be alone with them,

Kandy is their bait;

Equip yourself and

RUN – or The Junkyard is your fate.

4

Things Get Real

Mo

'Oh, bumbuckets.' I realised I was sweating, so I wiped my hands on my school trousers. 'Whoever left the envelope wants us to believe that there are Junkers in the world, Lottie. Junkers. Could this be real?'

'Let's think it through,' Lottie said. 'These Junkers are supposed to be evil bounty hunters...'

'Whose job is to get rid of unwanted people. And children.'

'Because there are too many children in the future,' she said.

'And they chop people up to use their parts.' I felt goosebumps prickle on my arms.

'Don't forget they use the parts themselves so they can change what they look like,' said Lottie.

'And they can travel in time,' I said, trying really hard to get my head around the explosion of information. 'What do you think? Is it true?'

'I have an instinct for these things, Mo, and

even though it is all a bit unusual, it actually makes sense.'

I nodded. It was crazy, but it fit.

'So they're here for us,' Lottie smiled, 'because we are so awesomely important.'

'They're here for us,' I repeated, not seeing why Lottie was smiling about it when I felt like I was going to puke.

'This changes everything,' Lottie said. 'We're in an actual life or death situation!'

'Well, a life or junk situation.'

'Any second, a Junker could come and fling us through space and time to a desolate wasteland, where we will spend the rest of our lives knowing our family will never find us.'

'We don't actually know it's a desolate wasteland, Lottie. It just said the Junkyard is in an unknown location.'

'Sure, sure. But the apocalyptic fallout zone part is implied. They're not going to send us to Disneyland, are they?'

'I suppose not.' My mouth was dry, probably because all the moisture in my body was being sweated out through my skin.

'It's probably a desert of black sand, with a

hungry monster who stalks the children, trying to catch its next meal.' Lottie was getting carried away again.

'Are you actually enjoying this, Lottie?' I asked.

'Kind of,' she said. 'I mean, I'm scared, but this all makes life so much more interesting. Besides, we'll obviously kick the bad guys' butts.'

'Will we?' I wished I had her confidence.

'Of course, Mo.' She put her arm around me. 'Don't worry. You're super-clever and I'm super-tough. We'll work it all out.'

'OK,' I said.

'I'm going to stop hugging you now, if that's OK, because you're also super-sweaty.'

'Let's look through the rest of the papers,' I said. 'Maybe there's something in here that will help us. Wait, what are you doing?'

'I'm changing my hair. If I'd known this was going to happen today, I would never have gone for a halo braid – it's completely inappropriate for this type of situation.'

'You're right,' I said. 'Lottie... would you do mine, too?'

Lottie gasped and squeaked simultaneously. 'OMG! Really, Mo?'

'Of course not,' I said. 'Because hair doesn't matter.'

'Aw, Mo, you made a joke. I'm proud of you.'

I leant over the papers so she couldn't see me smile.

Lottie

'So, what's next?' I said, as Mo turned to the next sheet.

'Nanotechnology,' Mo said. 'Why is this in here?'

It was a lot of information about how the idea for nanotechnology originated and developed.

'Nanotechnology is like making really powerful devices really, really tiny, right?' I said.

'Right,' Mo said, looking surprised that I would know something like that. Honestly, just because I care about other things, like hair and outfits, it doesn't mean I don't care about science and the world. If you turn to Exhibit K, you will see the first page of the Nanotech information. We haven't included the rest of it in the evidence box for reasons, aka – spoilers.

Nanotechnology is science, engineering and technology carried out on a teeny, tiny scale. Picture the smallest thing you can possibly imagine. What do you have in your head? An ant? A raindrop? A grain of sand? You need to think smaller. One nanometre is a billionth of a metre. A sheet of paper is 100,000 nanometres thick.

The concepts behind nanoscience were first talked about by physicist Richard Feynman, in 1959, when he described a process in which scientists would be able to manipulate and control individual atoms and molecules. The term 'nanotechnology' was coined many years later by Professor Norio Taniguchi.

The possibilities of working with materials on the nanoscale are endless, and have resulted in innovations in the fields of medicine, computing and engineering amongst others.

'Do you think this has something to do with the Discovery Competition? Maybe it's a clue to point us in the right direction.'

'Good thinking, Lottie,' Mo looked surprised again.

At the back of the Nanotech stuff, there was one final note. Please see Exhibit L:

WHAT COMES <u>NEXT</u>???!!

'You know, I really hate the way this guy punctuates,' Mo said. 'He's already underlined "NEXT". He only needs one question mark.'

'You get annoyed by the most ridiculous things, Mo. Exclamation mark, exclamation mark, exclamation mark,' I said. 'What does come next?'

'Well, we definitely need to rethink our Discovery Competition entry,' Mo said.

'Thank goodness you're finally agreeing with me. You know that's what I've been saying for DAYS.'

'I know, sorry, Lottie.'

'Apology accepted. So, we need something better, more imaginative, more exciting. We need to think big.'

'That's the thing – what the clue is trying to tell us,' Mo said. 'We don't need to think big, we need to think *small*.'

'Let's put all this away and we can brainstorm,' I said, sliding the papers back into the envelope.

'I'll put it in my secret box. It will be safe in there. Close your eyes so you can't see where I keep it.'

'Sure,' I said, knowing very well that it was under his bed. Bless Mo, so sweet and trusting. I'd looked through his secret box at least ten times already. I listened to him sliding the box out, pulling off the lid and then rummaging around inside.

'Something's wrong,' he said.

'What's wrong?'

'Have you been in my box?'

'Of course not, I don't even know where you keep it,' I lied. 'Why?'

'Something's missing. Something really important.'

'Can I open my eyes? I'll help you look.'

There was a moment of silence while Mo thought. 'OK,' he said.

'Ooh, look at all these things I've never seen before,' I used my best acting skills. Acting is one of my many talents. 'What's missing?'

'This thing I found at my old house, under the floorboards.'

'What does it look like?' I knew what it looked like.

'It's made of some kind of metal. It's square but rounded, and there's a hole in the middle.'

'Do you mean like a kind of square-shaped bracelet?' I asked as innocently as possible.

'Yes! Exactly! It has patterns on the outside, and I think it has some kind of tech inside. I've been trying to work out what it is. It's definitely gone.'

'Let me look,' I said, nudging him out of the way. I went through everything in his box, and the bracelet wasn't there. 'Maybe it fell out.'

We both crawled around the floor and under the bed, but we couldn't find it.

'I don't get it,' said Mo. 'Where could it have gone?'

'There's only one possible explanation. Somebody must have taken it.'

'Sadie,' Mo said.

'I don't think so, but let's check.'

'Sadie!' I yelled. 'Sadie!'

She appeared in the room without a sound. She was going to be a brilliant thief when she grew up.

'Did you take Mo's bracelet?' I asked. 'From his secret box?'

'Mew,' she shook her head.

'She said no, she didn't take your bracelet,' I said to Mo.

'Why should I believe her? And don't call it my bracelet. It makes me sound like a girl.'

'She'd tell me if she took it,' I said. 'And I haven't seen it in her box.'

'What do you mean? Have you looked in her secret box?'

'OMG, it's a secret box – of course I've looked in it. Why wouldn't I?'

'BECAUSE IT'S A SECRET BOX!' Mo shouted. 'Wait, have you looked in mine, too?'

'That's not important right now,' I said. 'Our priority is finding out who took your br– square-shaped metal arm thing.'

Sadie tugged on my sleeve. 'Perow mewt mewl.'

'Oh, that makes sense,' I said.

'What?' Mo said.

'You're not going to like it, Mo.'

'What, Lottie?'

'When Jax came up to use the bathroom earlier, Sadie saw him come in here.'

'So you're saying Jax took it?'

'That's exactly what I'm saying.'

'I don't know, Lottie.'

'Mo,' I said, 'it's time to face facts. Let's look at the evidence. One – Jax is new. He suddenly appeared and instantly tried to befriend you. Two – he's been asking strange questions and trying to put us off winning the Discovery Competition. Three – he wanted access to the school lost property and he was tearing through it like he was looking for something. Four – we don't know anything about him, he won't tell us where he lives and we've never seen his parents. And remember we heard a child's voice at Lorelai's house. Five – he's always eating sweets. Six – he had access to your bedroom and your secret box earlier today. Seven – the old school photo. I've looked at it a million times and I'm certain it's Jax. The clues are all there: befriending, sugar, time travel.'

'I've just realised something else,' Mo said, rooting through his box again. 'Look at this.'

He held up the Discovery Competition poster – the original one from class.

'What?' I said.

'Look at Jax's doodle.'

'OMG. It's the same as the patterns on your brace– decorated metal square with a hole.'

'How do you know that?' Mo frowned.

'I'm an excellent guesser,' I said. 'I'm right, aren't I?'

'Yes.'

'Jax is a Junker,' I said.

'Jax is a Junker. Probably.'

Making Plans on the Trampoline

Mo

'If he was going to all that trouble to find it, it must be important,' I said.

Lottie and I were sitting on the trampoline so we could talk in private.

'We have to do something,' Lottie said. 'He can't pretend to be your friend, then come over to our house and steal from us.'

'To be fair, the b– metal thing was probably his to start off with. Otherwise, how would he have known about it and why would he be looking for it?'

'Finders keepers, Mo.'

'That's not a thing, Lottie. Just because you find something, it doesn't make it yours.'

'So even if he's going to do evil things with it, you're OK with him having it because it technically belongs to him?' Lottie pulled the petals off a dandelion and threw them in the air.

'No,' I said. I didn't really know what was right.

'We've established that Jax is a Junker, yes?'

'Yes,' I said.

'And we're agreed that Junkers, who abduct children whose parents don't want them because they're a bit naughty and send them to a horrid place where they have to try to survive with no friends and no help – and let's not even get started on the "parts" part – are one hundred per cent bad?' She shuddered.

'Yes. Agreed.'

'So, what if the armband thing helps the Junkers to do their job, somehow? Are we just going to let him have it so he can junk innocent children?'

'No, I suppose not. You're right, we have to steal it back.'

'Right!' Lottie jumped up, making both of us wobble around on the trampoline. 'Let's go over to Lorelai's now. I'll create a diversion and you can sneak in.'

'I don't think that's the best way,' I said. 'We need to take our time and be careful. If we mess up, we won't get the holey, metal thing; Jax will know we're on to him and we might both be junked.'

'Ugh, I hate being patient,' Lottie said. 'Being

patient is for cows. Nobody ever got what they wanted by being patient.'

'That's so untrue, I don't even know where to start,' I said.

'What's your plan then, Mo?'

'I think we need to do this in stages. I'll get some paper and we can make a list.'

'Life on the edge. Hur-rah,' Lottie rolled her eyes.

I ignored her. Sometimes, with Lottie, it's the best way.

So we made an action plan – it's in the evidence box, labelled Exhibit R.

Mo and Lottie's Action Plan

Step 1: Find out where Jax lives.

Step 2: Find evidence that the Jax in photograph Exhibit E is the same Jax.

Step 3: Get Jax over to our house to see if he has the missing item in his pocket/in his bag/on his arm.

Step 4: If step 3 is unsuccessful, we will need to infiltrate his house. Assuming this is the house across the road, we will have to ensure nobody is home before we attempt to break in and retrieve the missing item.

Step 5: Find a better hiding place for the recovered item. Work out what it's for.

'We'd better make a blood pact,' Lottie said, 'So that we know we're in this together and will never betray each other.'

It sounded like something I probably wouldn't want to do. 'What's a blood pact?'

'We take a ceremonial knife, make small cuts on ourselves, squeeze drops of our blood into a sacred bowl, mix them together with an enchanted spoon and then drink the blood.'

'What? There's no way I'm doing that.'

'Why not? I said small cuts, Mo. Not big ones.' Lottie picked up a twig with a pointy end.

'What are you doing with that stick?' I backed away from her.

'Nothing,' she said. 'But just come here for a second, you've got something on your arm.'

'You're going to stab me with it!'

'Oh, Mo, you're such a baby,' she said, dropping the stick on the ground.

'How about we promise not to betray each other?' I said. 'We could swear on something we both care about.'

'OK, I swear on Schrodinger, not to betray you, Morris Appleby, and to work with you to defeat the Junkers.'

'I swear too,' I said.

She raised an eyebrow at me.

'To do the things that you just said to the best of my ability. Amen.'

'Ooh, we're stuck with each other now,' Lottie said.

Yay.

We started working on the plan the very next day that we were at school.

As usual, Jax came in a few minutes after everybody else. He looked tired. I wondered what Junkers got up to in their spare time and whether it involved late nights.

'Good morning, Jax,' Lottie said, in a really obviously sarcastic way.

'Hi,' I said to him, and managed to fake a small smile.

'Hey,' he said, and started picking at the edge of the table with his fingernail.

'More Discovery time, this morning, you lucky bag of jelly beans,' Mr Chartwell said. 'Separate into your groups and off you go – you should all be starting to make your prototypes by now.'

'Mo and I have been talking over the weekend,'

Lottie said, 'And we have decided that you're right, Jax. It's too late to start working on something new, so we're going to stick with the original idea.'

Jax didn't seem very interested. 'K.'

'So we'll go back into the storage room and keep going through the lost property,' I said. 'We've logged about half of it now.'

'You guys go,' Jax said. 'I'll stay here and work on the presentation to go with it.'

'Really?' Lottie said, 'But you always seem to love looking through the lost property. What's changed?'

She was being so obvious. I tried to give her a look, but she didn't notice.

'Nothing. Just it's really dusty in there and I have allergies,' Jax picked at the desk more viciously.

'You should have said something before,' Lottie said.

'It doesn't matter,' I gave Lottie another look. 'We'll go to the cupboard and you work here.'

Lottie and I got up and walked off. We were hardly even out of the door when she started doing that annoying loud whisper that people do, which is noisier than if they were talking in their normal voice. 'You see – he doesn't need to go through the storage cupboard now, because he's found what he was looking for! He's definitely one of them.'

'Shush, Lottie – he'll hear you!'

'You're letting him off too easily.'

'No, I'm trying not to blow our cover while we investigate. You're not helping.'

'It just makes me so angry!'

'I don't know, I still kind of feel sorry for him. He looks sad and poorly. Maybe he does have allergies.'

'Don't be ridiculous, Mo – he's a thief and a liar, remember?'

'I've got an idea about how we can get some more proof,' I said, to distract her from her angry ranting. 'But we're going to have to be a bit sneaky.'

'OMG. Do you mean we're going to break school rules?' Lottie squeaked.

'Yes. I've thought about it a lot and it's the only way.'

Lottie clapped her hands. 'Hurrah – you're finally turning to the dark side! I thought this day would never come. I'm so proud of you, Mo.'

'Shut up, Lottie. We're supposed to be sneaking.'

'Tell me, tell me, tell me!'

'OK, you know how there's a cupboard inside the lost-property cupboard, but it's locked?'

'We're breaking in, aren't we? We're. Breaking. In!'

'We're not breaking in,' I said.

'Disappointing.'

'We have the key. It's right here next to the main cupboard key.'

'But Mo, they're trusting us with those keys,' Lottie said.

'I know. I feel bad, but it has to be done.'

'Well, this is like the best day ever!' Lottie grinned. 'What's in the other cupboard?'

'Old school records, from before they put everything on the computer. They used to keep paper copies, you know. In the olden days.'

'How wasteful.'

'I know. Anyway, I'm hoping we can find the names and addresses of pupils from previous years.'

'Like ten years ago, for example?'

'Exactly.'

We opened the main storage cupboard and

pulled the door behind us so that it was almost shut. I held the second key on the ring, and tried it in the lock of the dusty cabinet that stood in the corner.

'I don't think I've ever liked you as much as I do in this moment, Mo,' Lottie said. 'This is special.'

'Don't be stupid, Lottie,' I said, but I was smiling on the inside of my face.

The key went into the hole and the lock turned. The cabinet was open.

'So. Much. Paper,' Lottie groaned.

'We'd better get started, then.' I pulled out a file and opened it.

Following Jax

Mo

When we went back to class an hour later, we hadn't found anything. There was a lot to go through and we'd run out of time, but I was hopeful that we'd get another chance to look.

Jax was weird all day. He went off on his own a lot and he hardly spoke. Whatever Lottie said about him, I couldn't help but think he wasn't completely evil. I found it hard pretending to be friendly, while we were plotting behind his back.

At the end of the day, we put the second part of our plan into action. Instead of rushing out of the door as soon as Mr Chartwell said it was home time, Lottie and I hid in the toilets.

'Should we hide together, or separately?' Lottie said.

'I don't mind.'

'Let's hide together. In the boys' toilets – I've always wanted to go in there.'

'Weird.'

We shut ourselves in a cubicle and waited.

Usually at the end of school, if we waited for Jax, he would realise he'd forgotten something and go running back to our classroom, telling us to go without him. It was like he wanted to make sure we'd left before he went home. Today was going to be different.

We snuck out of the toilets and made our way to the exit by our classroom. There were a few kids left in the playground – the younger ones whose mums were running late. The rule is that after ten minutes, any kids who hadn't been collected were taken to the office to wait while Miss Woods phoned their mums.

As we'd suspected, Jax was standing on the corner, waiting to make sure the playground was clear before he left. We watched him peep around the side of the building before he made his way down the path. Once he was at the gates, he looked both ways. We hid behind the wall until he turned right up the road, and then we followed.

'This is so exciting!' whispered Lottie.

Jax was walking the opposite way to the direction we always walked in. I started to wonder if we'd got him wrong. I started to *hope* we'd got him wrong. When he reached the end of the road, he turned left up the hill, past the green. The green had lots of big trees all around it, so it was easy for us to keep behind him without being seen. As we dodged from tree to tree, I had to admit (to myself, obviously – not out loud), that Lottie was right: it was exciting.

Once we were past the green, it was trickier. The road was long and straight, so we had to stay a good distance back and keep running into people's gardens. After about a hundred metres, Jax paused and turned. Lottie grabbed me and threw me into a bush.

'Did he see us?' I said.

'I don't think so.'

We stayed there for a moment, out of breath. Following a potential Junker home from school is much harder work than you'd think. I peeped around the bush and couldn't see Jax anywhere.

'Quick!' I said, 'He's gone!'

We ran as fast as we could up the road, knowing he must have gone into one of the houses, or turned off down another road.

'This. Is. Living!' Lottie whooped as we flew along.

As we reached a turning, I realised where Jax

had gone. I turned left again and there he was in the distance. He was walking down Morello Road. He'd gone in a big circle and come to it from the other end.

'Oh, he is so going to your old house, Mo,' Lottie said.

I had a horrible feeling that she was right.

We watched him walk down the hill towards our houses. Just before he reached them, he turned into the little sidestreet, and then into the alley that led to the garden of my old house.

'There's no denying it, then,' I said, as he unlocked the gate and went in.

Lottie

The first thing I thought when I saw Jax the next day was that I wanted to punch him in the face. The second thing I thought was that Mo really didn't look angry enough.

'What's the matter, Mo?' I asked.

'Nothing,' he said.

'We should be able to get into those files again today. Maybe we'll find what we're looking for.'

'Yes, maybe,' he sighed.

Jax started walking towards us.

'Time to put my amazing acting skills to good use,' I said to Mo, and I covered my face with the best fake smile anyone has ever seen.

'Hi, guys,' Jax said. 'How are you doing?'

'Perfectly wonderful,' I said.

'How are you, Jax?' said Mo.

'I'm alright,' he said and looked down at his feet.

'Do you want to come over after school?' Mo asked.

'That would be nice, if you're sure it's OK,' Jax said.

Honestly, everybody was being awfully polite. It was very strange.

'Absolutely,' I smiled.

'Do you want to work with us in the storage cupboard today?' Mo said. I jabbed him in the belly with my elbow.

'Jax has *allergies*, remember, Mo? Anyway, we need him to keep writing out the description of our invention. You don't mind staying here, do you Jax?'

'No, I don't mind. You guys go ahead.'

'Thanks so much, Jax – you are such a sweetheart,' I said, as I pulled Mo out of the classroom.

'Don't you think you're going a bit over the top, Lottie?' Mo said.

'The question we should be asking here is don't you think you're going a bit under the bottom, Mo? Why did you ask him to come with us to the cupboard?'

'I don't know. I felt a bit sorry for him.'

'We need to stick to the plan!'

'I know. I just…'

'At least we know who the weak link is on our team! You need to toughen up, Mo. You don't see the baby antelopes in South America asking the lion who wants to eat them to join them in their nest!'

'That's because there aren't any antelopes or lions in South America! And they don't live in a nest!' Mo went bright red.

'You know what I mean, Mo Appleby. Now, girl up and let's get on and find the file.'

I know I was being harsh on him, but he really was too kind-hearted for his own good.

After thirty minutes in the cabinet, we finally found what we were looking for: the pupil files from ten years ago.

'I don't know what name to look for, and we're running out of time,' Mo said.

'We need to narrow it down a bit. See if you can find the class lists, then there will only be about thirty names, and half of those will be girls.'

'Good thinking, Lottie,' Mo said, with an unmistakable tone of surprise.

'I've got it!' I said, continuing my run of continuing to demonstrate my extremely impressive investigational skills. 'Let's see – Year 6…'

We looked down the list together, but I spotted it first. Please see Exhibit M – the old class list for Year 6 in St Pippin's Primary.

Annika Allen	18 Morello Road
Aidan Bedford-Nuttall	12 Sycamore Street
Theo Bennett	259 Gwenver Road
Chase Bermingham	28 Fairfield Road
Peggy Callaghan	39 Rose Avenue
Madeline Rose Caunt	3 Summer Street
Summer Davis	14 Rose Avenue
Charlie Ferrier	159 Morello Road
Luke Gormley	5 Durham Court
Archie Hankey	64 Stanley Road
Michael Ing	42 Quince Way
Holly Long	77 Snow Street

Lotti Long	77 Snow Street
Edward Marsh	1 Valentine Lane
Rhys McInnes	6 Fournier Drive
Jack Melvin	79 Morello Road
Laura Murray	92 Colham Road
Asha Raj	21 Plumstead Street
Charlotte Edie Read	155 Sycamore Street
Todd Siegert	1 Gwenver Road
Sheriynta Silas	8 Horseshoe Lane
Nia Talbot	29 Mabel Avenue
Christian Wylie	5 Bliss Lane
Tonicha Upham	15 Willow Walk
Jemima West	118 Iris Road
Danny Wright	9 Mayland Drive
Reyhan Younis	33 Kestrel Way
Isaac Zizinga	183 Franklin Road

'Jack Melvin! It sounds so similar to Jax Melville. It has to be him!'

'You're right, Lottie, it must be! And look at the address: 79 Morello Road.'

'Your old house.'

'He lived there before Mum moved there.'

'He hid the metal thing under the floorboard.'

'He forgot it when they left.'

'And he came back to find it,' I said. 'And to get rid of us, of course.'

'I wonder why they were here before?' Mo said.

'Maybe they were after somebody else. I almost feel sorry for Jax – can you imagine having to go through the same year at school over and over again? How incredibly boring.'

'You know, I don't think I'd mind that. You'd know what you were doing and things wouldn't keep changing,' Mo said. 'It would be quite nice.'

'You're so weird. If Jax has been to school a hundred times before, you'd think he'd be more helpful with our Discovery project. He must have seen loads of good science experiments.'

'He's only interested in finding what he's lost.'

'So selfish,' I sighed.

'It must be really important to him. Remember how we felt when Schrodinger went missing? We couldn't think about anything except getting him back.'

'That was different. Schrodinger is part of our family – losing him would be the worst.'

'That's what we could do for the Discovery competition!' Mo said. 'We could invent something to stop people from losing their pets.

What about a tiny device you can attach to your cat that allows you to track where it is on your phone, or laptop?'

'That is actually a brilliant idea.'

'So, shall we work on it together?'

'I'd really like that. We'd better keep it a secret from Jax, though.'

'I hate keeping secrets,' Mo sighed. 'It feels like lying.'

'Don't wimp out on me now, Mo. He's supposed to be coming over, remember? We have to be fake nice to him, at least for the rest of today.'

Pretending with Jax

Lottie

At home time, Jax walked out with us, looking very pleased with himself, but I was distracted from being annoyed by another big scene at the crossing.

The lollipop man was standing in the middle of the road, facing a group of secondary school kids who were all laughing and shouting rude things at him.

He planted his feet shoulder-width apart and banged the end of his stick down on the ground. 'You shall not pass.'

'You're not the crossing police, we can go across whenever we like,' one of the teenagers sniggered at him, while another threw a bit of his sausage roll. Luckily, because Hector's coat was made of yellow plasticky stuff, it just bounced off without leaving a mark. But it obviously peed him off.

'YOU SHALL NOT PASS!'

'Is he trying to be Gandalf?' Mo said, smiling. I think he actually thought it was cool.

'He's absolutely mental,' I said.

'He's nuts,' Jax agreed.

'I like him,' said Mo. 'He's funny.'

'Come on, let's just cross or we'll be here all night,' I said, and we walked quickly over the crossing with a big group of other kids, leaving Hector to his bonkers stand-off.

It was late October and starting to get colder but, for some reason, I really wanted ice cream. I knew it was weird, but once the idea had popped into my head, I was powerless to stop it.

'Shall we walk the long way around and look for Mr Gideon?' I said.

'We've got stuff to do, remember?' Mo gave me a cross look.

'It will only take a few extra minutes, and then Jax can have an ice cream, too.'

'It would be good to have an ice cream, I suppose,' Mo said, turning to take the long cut home.

'To be honest, I really need to pee.' Jax stopped walking. 'Can we go straight to yours? I'm desperate.'

How disappointing. Anyone would have thought he didn't want an ice cream. He really didn't know what he was missing.

'If we must,' I said, feeling extremely annoyed.

I listened out for 'Who's Afraid of the Big Bad Wolf?' all the way home, but there was no sign of Mr Gideon.

When we got home, Emma seemed thrilled. 'How lovely to see you again, Jax! How are you?'

'I'm OK, thank you,' he smiled and his cheeks turned pink.

'Can I get you something to drink? Some snacks, too? What would you like?'

'Yes please, erm, Mrs...'

'Just call me Emma, sweetheart.'

'OK, thanks, Emma.'

Emma went into the kitchen and made up a big tray of juice and snacks. 'Are you lot going upstairs to work?'

'Actually, I could do with a break,' I said. 'Let's play in the garden.'

Mo opened the back door and we took the tray outside. While Mo and Jax started eating, I ran into the house to get Sadie.

'Sadie, we need your expertise,' I said. 'You know the thing we discussed?'

She nodded.

'It's time.'

She cracked her knuckles and followed me to the garden.

We played until dinner, and then we sat and watched TV. Jax was being different from usual. He was quiet and shy, but didn't seem in a rush to go home. I couldn't tell if it was an act or not.

At seven-thirty, he got a text, which must have been from his mum, because he jumped up saying he had to go.

'Let me take you home, Jax,' Emma said. 'Where do you live?'

'No, thank you – my mum's outside.'

'Are you sure? I don't like you leaving on your own when it's dark.'

'Yes, I'm sure.' He grabbed his jacket and bag and ran for the door. 'Thanks for dinner, Emma!' he yelled, and closed the front door behind him.

'I'm just going upstairs to do some homework,' I said, winking at Mo.

'That's good,' he said and kept watching TV.

'I might need your help, though,' I said, in the most subtly obvious voice I could.

'Do it here, then, and I'll help you while I'm watching.'

'Mew,' Sadie looked at Mo and shook her head.

'Mo, darling,' Emma looked up from her book. 'I think Lottie wants to talk to you in private.'

'Meowt,' said Sadie.

'And Sadie does, too.'

Emma was such a cool mum, I was getting very attached to her. I might even be sad to leave her when Mum came back for us.

'Oh, right,' said Mo. 'Thanks, Mum.' He gave her a hug and she ruffled his hair. It made me feel a bit funny – sort of sad and happy at the same time. But I had more important things to worry about.

'We really need some kind of secret code – a password or hand gesture or something.'

'Why?' said Mo.

'So we can communicate without other people knowing what we're saying. For example, if I want you to come for an emergency Junker meeting upstairs.'

'Mum didn't care anyway,' Mo said.

'As always, Mo, you are completely missing the point.'

When we were safely in Mo's room with the door closed, I turned to Sadie.

'Did you find the metal arm thing?' I said.

While we'd been playing, Sadie had searched

Jax's bag, jacket and trouser pockets for the bracelet he stole, and anything else that might help us to get one step ahead of the Junkers.

'Purow,' Sadie shook her head.

'Oh, fluff, I forgot about that,' Mo said.

'How could you have forgotten? That was the whole reason we invited him over!'

'I know, but it was kind of fun, and it slipped my mind.'

'You need to focus, Mo! This is life or death stuff, remember?'

'You're right. I just find the pretending thing hard. I'm sorry.'

'Jax didn't have the armband on him.' I said. 'Was there anything else, Sades?'

Sadie reached down the back of her pants and pulled out a scrap of paper that looked like it had been ripped out of a St Pippins creative-writing journal. Take a look at Exhibit X:

The Junkyard by Jax Melville

There is a place I see in my nightmares. It is an island, surrounded by the angry seas whose depths are full of lurking shadows. There are no boats. There is only one way to leave.

The island is in ruins. Most of it burnt and crumbling like charcoal, the few bildings still standing are relics from another time. It is frozen in the past and the future.

The only things that grow there are brown grasses and tough, scratchy vines which creep over evrything. They look like tentacles trying to pull the ruins down into the earth.

The sky is always grey and full of thunder. There are storms so loud they make me shake. Creetures prowl, especialy at night. They aren't like the animals we know. They began that way – as gorillas and tigers and crocodiles in the zoo. But then the walls fell down and the animals escaped. Over years they have evolved. They had to or they wouldn't have survived. Now they are terrible beasts who growl and stalk and hunt. They are always hungry.

Near the center of the island is a prison. Missing people are taken there – children who dissapeared on there way home from school, men and women who went for a walk one day and never made it home. Most of them are good. And they are kept locked up in the darkness. There is no escape.

162

'All those years of school haven't made him a good speller,' I said. 'And the Junkyard sounds like a lovely place.'

'How can you say that, Lottie? It sounds awful!'

'It's called sarcasm, Mo.'

'Oh. Do you think it's about the real Junkyard?' Mo said.

'It seems unlikely that it's just a coincidence.'

'Right,' said Mo.

'Yeah,' I said. 'What are we going to do now?'

'We'll just have to move to the next stage of our plan,' Mo said. 'We'll have to get into the house, somehow.'

'Well neither of us is going to fit through the cat flap, if that's what you're thinking.'

'Perow mewl prrr,' said Sadie, and she pulled something out of her pocket.

'Is that what I think it is?' Mo said.

'Jax's keys.' I grinned.

'Sadie, you are the most talented four-year-old I've ever met,' Mo said. 'You're going to be a master criminal one day.'

Sadie giggled and kissed Mo's arm.

Thanks to Sadie, getting into the Junker house wasn't going to be as difficult as we thought. We just needed to get them out of the way…

Time for Action

Mo

The next part of the plan was by far the trickiest and most likely to lead to injury or junking. I was nervous about it but, when I thought about the poor kids being abducted by the Junkers, I knew it was the right thing to do. We had to find a way to get the armband back.

Lottie's idea was to go running over to the Junker house and hope for the best. I persuaded her that we would stand a much better chance with a bit of preparation. The day before our planned infiltration, we took a detour on the way home from school. To the post office. It might not sound very butt-kicking, but it was an essential part of the plan.

'Why are you two late home?' Mum said when we walked through the door.

'There was a food sale after school, to raise money for dogs with two legs,' Lottie said. I usually left the lying to her – she was so much better at it than I was.

'Oh, that's an unusual charity,' Mum frowned and hung our coats up for us.

'Dogs with two legs need our compassion, Emma. Imagine how hard it is for them. The money goes towards building them tiny wheelchairs.'

'Of course. I didn't mean to be insensitive. What food did you eat at the sale?'

'Oh, all sorts,' Lottie said. 'Cakes and cheese and this strange meat that tasted a bit funny.'

'Sounds delicious,' Mum said.

'It was, wasn't it, Mo?'

I nodded.

'We're going upstairs to work on our Discovery Competition entry,' I said.

'Alright, my loves, I'll call you down when dinner's ready.'

'Can we eat in my room today? We have so much work to do.'

'I suppose that would be OK,' Mum said. 'As it's for something so important. I'll bring you up some trays.'

'Thanks, Mum. You're the best.'

Up in my room, we really did work on our invention. I was putting together a prototype, while Lottie was writing our presentation.

'It's way too big,' I said. 'It needs to be a thousand times smaller. It's not good enough.'

'Mo, it's just a prototype to give the judges an idea of what the final product will be. Plus, you're ten years old and you just built a tracking device out of bits of broken phones. I think they're going to be impressed.'

'But I don't know if it's enough to win.'

'I've been snooping around looking at the other teams' inventions and they're a big pile of poop compared to ours. Just make sure it works and I'll take care of the rest.'

'What do you mean by "the rest"?'

'Oh, you know, the market research, the branding, the sales pitch…'

'It isn't *Junior Apprentice*, Lottie.'

'Of course it is, Mo. Cherry Corp aren't just investing in the invention; they're investing in the inventors. We need to show them how awesome we are.'

'It's not going to involve costumes, is it?' I asked.

'Mo, we're professionals – we can't be wearing silly outfits. We'll be wearing something appropriate. Maybe with new hairstyles…' she side-eyed me.

'No,' I said.

'We'll discuss it later. Anyway, I've been thinking about product names. We want something catchy. Maybe something that ties in with the Cherry Corp brand.'

'It's called a Pet-Tracker, and the viewing software is called The Trace.'

'I see two problems with your names, Mo,' Lottie said. 'Firstly, you're not thinking of the bigger picture. By calling it a Pet-Tracker you're limiting our market to just pets, when it could be used for other things.'

'What other things are likely to go missing?'

'OMG – that's it, Mo! Children: children are likely to go missing in the future. What if, one day, our tracker can be used on people, to stop them from getting lost or disappearing?'

She was right. She'd cracked it. That must be what all this stuff was about – the thing we were yet to do that would lead us into danger, the reason why the Junkers wanted to get rid of us. It had to be!

'That's possible, I suppose,' I said. 'But we're nowhere near being able to use the tracker in that way.'

'We don't have to be. This is just the start – we have years to work on it. I just think we should give it more of a multi-use name. What exactly is it again?'

'It's a massive, messy ball of parts at the moment, but one day I want it to be an implantable positioning system. And it needs to be tiny – smaller than nanotech.'

'What's smaller than nanotech?'

'I don't think there's a word for it yet... Maybe picotech?'

'So, how about this: Picotechnological Implantable Positioning System. They can be called PIPS for short, which works because they're so tiny.'

'That's quite good, actually,' I said.

'Ooh, ooh, and it goes with Cherry Corp. Cherry – pips. You see?'

'Can we keep The Trace, though? I like that.'

'Absolutely not. What sort of a name is The Trace? It sounds like a gameshow. Nobody's going to remember something like that.'

She kept bobbing on for a while, but I stopped listening and got on with making the device.

A while later, Mum brought up our dinner

trays and then went downstairs to eat with Spencer and Sadie.

'Spaghetti Bolognese,' Lottie smiled. 'Perfect.'

'Can we at least eat some of it?' It smelled so good.

'We can eat most of it. Just leave like a big handful.'

'It seems as if you've done this before,' I said.

'Don't worry, Mo – you are in expert hands.'

We ate most of our dinners, leaving a large dollop each, which we mashed up with our forks and poured into cups. Lottie went into the bathroom and filled the cups with water, and then we stirred the mixtures until we had a bolognesey-soupy-mush.

'Are you ready?' Lottie said, hiding her cup.

I nodded and filled my mouth with the bolo-puke.

'Emma!' Sadie called, 'Can you come up? Mo's not feeling well!'

Mum ran up the stairs just as I spat the bolo-puke into the toilet, making lots of sicky noises at the same time.

'Oh, Mo-Bear!' Mum gave me some tissue and felt my head. 'When did you start feeling sick?'

'I don't know,' I said. I felt really guilty about

lying to her. 'It might have been that meat we ate at the food sale. It did taste strange.'

'Do you need to be sick again, or do you want to have a lie-down?'

'Lie down, I think,' I said, letting Mum lead me to my room.

'Actually,' Lottie called from the bathroom, 'I think I might be...' And she spat her bolo-puke into the toilet, too, doing the most over-the-top puking noises I've ever heard.

'Oh god,' Mum said. 'Spencer! Can you come up, please? Lottie's sick!'

'Really sick or fake sick?' Spencer called back. He was so much more clued up about Lottie than Mum was.

'Really, *really* sick,' Mum said.

Mum and Spencer got me and Lottie dressed in our pyjamas and into bed with glasses of water and buckets next to us. I had to hand it to Lottie – her part of the plan had worked perfectly.

The next morning, Mum came into my room and stroked my forehead.

'How are you feeling, lovely?'

'Much better,' I said. 'Do you think I should go to school?'

'Not today, Mo-Bear. I'm not allowed to send you back until at least twenty-four hours after you were last sick. I'm sorry.'

'It's OK, Mum, I understand.'

'You and Lottie can stay home today and snuggle up in front of the telly. Do you think you can manage anything to eat?'

'Maybe something small to start off with,' I said.

'Good boy – I'll get you some dry toast and we'll see if you keep it down.'

Five minutes later, Lottie came in. 'I told you it would work,' she said. 'With Jax safely at school, that's one less Junker to worry about.'

'The next part is up to Sadie – do you think she'll get it right?'

'Of course. Sadie is very good at that type of thing. She won't let us down.'

Lottie and I got dressed and worked on our invention while we waited for the right moment.

At 10 am, Mum called up, 'Mo! Lottie! I'm just popping over to Lorelai's to see if she wants to come over for a coffee.'

'Why's that, Emma?' Lottie said, as we made our way down the stairs.

'Sadie saw her looking out of the window and thinks she's lonely. She very kindly suggested we invite her over. Isn't she a sweetie-pie?'

'Being sweet is Sadie's third best quality,' Lottie said.

'I'll be back in two minutes.' Mum went out of the front door.

We watched from the window as she rang the Junkers' doorbell and Lorelai answered. They spoke for a moment, then Lorelai did one of her Disney smiles and came out of her house, pulling the door closed behind her.

'We'll be in the kitchen, you two,' Mum said as she walked through the house with Lorelai. 'I'll keep Lorelai out of your way, just in case you're contagious – we wouldn't want her getting sick, would we?'

'If I really was contagious, I'd go and lick her coffee cup,' said Lottie.

She was so much better at being bad than I was.

We went back to the window and waited. At 10:12am, the postman walked up to Lorelai's front door and rang the bell. Our postman always got to 79 Morello Road at between 10:10am and 10:18am. I knew this because I used to wait at the door for my Lego Club magazines to arrive.

'You were right, Mo,' Lottie said. 'It was worth spending £7 on that parcel.'

At the post office the day before, we'd paid for special delivery on an empty box we'd wrapped in brown paper and addressed to Lorelai.

'Now we'll see if anyone else is home,' I said.

The postman rang again, and rattled the letterbox, but there was no movement from the house. Eventually, he left a card and moved on.

'Are you ready?' I said, suddenly feeling nervous.

'Totes.'

We told Mum we were going upstairs to chill out, and then we snuck out of the front door. Sadie was on distraction duty but we didn't know how much time we'd have. Our aim was to go in, find the armband thing within a few minutes, and get out again. No messing.

We ran down the alley and I lifted the loose planks in the fence so that Lottie could slip through.

'All clear,' she said, and I followed.

As we raced to the back door, I pulled Jax's keys out of my pocket and slotted the smaller one into the lock. It turned with a clunk.

'Quiet, Mo!' Lottie whispered.

'How am I supposed to make a lock turn quietly?'

'Are you telling me you haven't been practising?'

'Of course I haven't been practising. I've had other things to do, like inventing a device that will change the future of the world.'

'Well, if the job of opening the door had been assigned to me, *I* would have practised doing it quietly.'

'But you're making more noise arguing about it than the lock made in the first place!' I was getting cross.

'Well, why are you talking then, Mo?'

I swore inside my head and tried to focus on the task.

The door swung open.

Into the Junkers' Lair

Lottie

I could tell Mo was really nervous, so I tried to help by talking him through everything, but as we stepped into the house it suddenly all seemed extremely serious, so I chatted to keep myself from freaking out.

'I see they haven't tidied up, then,' I said, looking round at the piles of electrical junk.

'I wish I could look at what they're building with this stuff.' Mo wandered around, poking at things. 'This could be for time travel – imagine how much I could learn!'

'Well, we don't have time,' I said, pulling him into the hallway. 'And anyway, it would be cheating to look at technology that hasn't even been invented yet.'

'You're right. I'd much rather do things my own way,' Mo said.

'Oh, really – I would never have guessed that about you.'

'What's that supposed to mean?'

'Focus, Mo: where are we looking first?'

'My old room,' he said, running up the stairs. Mo looks really funny when he runs, because he's so sturdy and his legs are short. He's like a little boulder with feet.

He opened the first door on the right and I followed him into a small bedroom.

'Oh,' he said.

The room was bare. There was no carpet or rugs on the floor; no cupboards or drawers or boxes of stuff. There wasn't even a bed, just a mattress on the floor. Jax's clothes were crumpled in a heap in one corner. It was the most pathetic-looking bedroom I'd ever seen.

'He doesn't have much stuff, does he?' Mo said.

'He only has, like, two outfits.'

'No books or games.'

'I suppose if you're constantly time-travelling, you don't stay in one place long enough to bother making it nice,' I said.

'This sucks,' Mo frowned. 'Poor Jax.'

'No, no, no, Mo Appleby – you are not allowed to feel sorry for Jax Melville! He lied to us, remember? And stole from us. And he helps his parents abduct children and send them to a nightmarish land where only the strongest survive. He deserves this.'

'I guess,' Mo said, but he didn't look convinced.

'Find the metal arm thing, Mo.'

'Right. Yes.' He went over to a corner of the room and pulled up a loose floorboard. 'Damn, it isn't here! I was so sure this is where it would be.'

It was extremely disappointing after all the trouble we'd gone to.

'We have a few minutes,' I said. 'Let's quickly look around the house. We know he doesn't have it on him, because Sadie checked.'

'But maybe he has it today. Or maybe Lorelai has it.'

'Then Sadie will get it.'

We ran to the bathroom, looking in the cabinet and behind the toilet. It wasn't there. The only other room upstairs was what must have once been Emma's bedroom but was now Lorelai's. Mo shoved the door open and ran into the room ahead of me. He stopped so suddenly that I crashed into him.

'What the heck, Mo?' I shouted, before I realised what had glued him to the floor.

On a long table in front of us there was a row of

white plastic heads, and on each head was a wig. Every wig was different – a straight brown bob, dark red ringlets, black braids. I crept forward and touched the hair.

'I think this is real,' I whispered.

'That's disgusting.' Mo took a step back.

'I've always wondered what I'd look like with straight hair,' I said, putting on the brown bob.

'Take it off, Lottie!'

'I'm coming to rub my wig on you, Mo! I said and started chasing him around the room. You should have seen Mo's face – he was horrified. Unfortunately, I tripped on a box that was poking out from under the bed, and the wig fell off, and landed upside down on the floor.

'That's weird,' Mo said, peering at it. 'I think it's made from real skin.'

'You mean I just had someone else's hair and skin flakes on my head?' I asked, feeling sick.

'I think you did,' Mo said, looking like he was about to puke.

I've never been so disgusted in my life, but I didn't want Mo to see. 'Oh well – YOLO,' I said, putting the disgusting thing back onto its plastic head.

'We'd better check the box,' said Mo, bending down to pull it from under the bed.

'Can't be worse than the wigs,' I said, undoing the clasp and lifting the lid.

Inside was what looked like rows and rows of different coloured marbles, all lined up in sets of two.

'What could these be?' Mo said, picking one up and rolling it between his fingers.

'Mo,' I said. 'They're eyeballs.'

'Oh, buttgubbins!' Mo dropped the eyeball and it rolled across the floor.

'Quick, Mo, get it back or Lorelai will know someone's been here!'

Mo crawled quickly across the carpet and stopped the eyeball with the sleeve of his jumper, which he'd pulled down over his hand.

'It's got bits of fluff stuck on it,' he wailed. 'What do I do?'

'You'll have to pick it off, quick,' I said, rather enjoying the sound of Mo heaving and retching.

'I can't. I can't do it,' he said, with tears in his eyes. 'I know, I'll rinse it under the tap!'

He ran to the bathroom and turned on the water. When he returned with the eyeball, it was glistening with drops of water.

'It'll dry before she sees it,' Mo said, trying to put it back into the box with as little skin-on-eyeball contact as possible.

'It's the wrong way round, Mo. It's looking at you,' I said. 'Hi there – I'm Mister Eyeball and I know what you've done, Mo Appleby.'

Mo turned it round, slammed the box shut and pushed it back under the bed. 'I've had enough of this room,' he said. 'Let's look downstairs.'

We couldn't find the bracelet in the kitchen, either. 'This is disgusting,' I said, pointing to a piece of mouldy cheese and half a bottle of lumpy milk, which were the only food items in the whole kitchen. The bin was full, though, of crisp packets and cereal boxes, and chocolate wrappers.

'I don't think they eat very well,' Mo said. 'No wonder Jax likes having dinner at ours.'

'No wonder he eats so much when he has dinner at ours.'

'Poo–'

'Honestly, Mo, if you're going to say "Poor Jax" again, I'm going to punch you right in the mouth.'

'We'd better go,' Mo said. 'We've been here too long.'

'What a waste of time.' I felt utterly crushed. I'd been so sure we'd get that bracelet back.

'I know! The cupboard under the stairs!' Mo said, and we ran into the hallway again.

He flung the door open, to reveal a dusty, dark cupboard.

'Fluff,' he said.

And then the sound of the lock turning in the back door made us jump. Someone was coming into the house.

'Quick!' I threw Mo into the cupboard and pulled the door shut behind us, just as the back door slammed and footsteps thumped through the house.

We sat, huddled in the cupboard, hardly daring to breathe as the footsteps came closer. The air in the cupboard was freezing cold and smelt of old things, and the floor was covered in bits of grit, or sawdust. I was worried the Junker had seen us closing the door. I was worried I might sneeze because of all the dust. I was worried there might be spiders.

'Just get back, quick,' a gruff man's voice said. My heart pounded so hard in my chest that I thought it might burst through my ribcage and explode all over Mo. 'I've got some more parts I need you to sort through.'

It was OK. He was on the phone. The good news was that he didn't appear to know we were there. The bad news was that we would soon have two Junkers to get past, instead of just one. We had to get out.

It was too dark in the cupboard to see Mo's face, so I fumbled around and grabbed his hand. He squeezed mine tightly back, and I felt a little less afraid. As the Junker walked upstairs and the footsteps thundered over our heads, I think we both knew it was our only chance.

Mo shoved open the cupboard door and we ran to the kitchen, as quickly and quietly as we could. The back door wasn't properly shut, so all we had to do was give it a gentle push and we were out into the garden, blinking in the bright sunlight.

We dashed to the fence, not daring to look behind us. Mo made it there first (he was surprisingly fast for a boulder with legs).

'Go, go!' I said and he squeezed through the gap, then held the planks aside for me. As I crawled through the hole, I was sure I could feel hot breath on my legs and I expected at any moment someone to grab me and drag me back to the Junker house. I have to tell you, it was an incredibly unpleasant sensation. I thought I might even pee myself.

At the last second, there was a pull on my foot. I kicked out as hard as I could, in a desperate panic, but I couldn't get my foot through the hole.

'It's OK, Lottie,' Mo said, stretching his arm towards me. 'Your sock is caught on the fence, that's all. Stay still and I'll unsnag it.'

I tried my hardest to be still and calm like an otter while Mo unhooked my sock. We slid the planks back into place and turned into the alley, almost running bang into a van that was parked by the gate. A van that hadn't been there before.

An ice cream van.

'Mr Gideon,' Mo said. 'The ice cream.'

'Mo, we have to go!' I screamed. Even though Mr Gideon's ice cream was ridiculously good, nothing could have made me stay by that Junker house. We started running down the alley, but as we reached a slight bend in the path, I saw movement ahead.

I stopped, suddenly. 'Lorelai's coming!'

'Has she seen us?'

'I don't think so – not yet.'

'Where do we go? WHERE DO WE GO?'

We backed up towards the Junker house where we could hear the metal latch on the gate being lifted.

'He's coming out,' I gasped.

We were trapped.

'The van,' said Mo. 'It's our only chance.' He pulled on the back doorhandle, and it creaked open.

'Oh god, we really don't want to do this,' I said.

'We really have to,' Mo panted, as he pushed me in and closed the door behind us. Just in time.

Footsteps crunched on the gravel by the van. 'Where have you been?' said the growly Junker voice, which apparently was Mr Gideon's.

'Across the road with that idiotic woman and her bizarre stepdaughter,' Lorelai said. 'She was insisting on showing me dance routines and magic tricks – such a talentless child. It's hard to believe that the family is such a threat to us.'

I really wanted to get out of the van and tell Lorelai how ghastly her weird tight face and wrinkly neck were, but Mo put his hand on my arm. 'If we get out of this van, it'll be over,' he said.

He was right.

'I take it the kids are still enjoying your ice cream?' Lorelai said. I could hear the nasty smile in her voice.

'Of course – same as all the others – they just can't keep away. If we need to grab one from the street it won't be hard to get close.' Mr Gideon laughed.

'Are the parts in the van?' Lorelai said, and there was a tap on the back doors, as though she was going to open them. There was nowhere to hide inside the van. We were doomed. A grisly and horrific death awaited us. I was surprised – I'd always thought I'd make it to at least the age of twenty-five. I deserved that – to grow up and be able to wear T-shirts with inappropriate slogans on them. To get my nose pierced. To run the London marathon dressed as an astronaut. This was terribly unfair.

'I've already taken them inside,' Mr Gideon said, and the door didn't open.

Mo let out a breath he had clearly been holding for a while. His cheeks were so red they made his hair look dull. I wondered what he'd been worrying about missing out on if he died young.

'Thanks, handsome,' Lorelai said.

Gross. I looked at Mo and he wrinkled his nose in disgust.

'I've got to go and collect another load, and then I'll be in to help,' Mr Gideon said. 'See you later, princess.'

There was a slight squelching sound, which I think was them kissing. It was just awful.

Then the gravel crunched, the door by the driver's seat swung open, and the van dipped as Mr Gideon got in. We were trapped. Again.

Soon we were bouncing down the alley and bumping about every time the van went over a pothole.

'How are we going to get out?' I whispered to Mo.

'We'll have to wait until he stops, and then run.'

'But we might be miles away by then.'

'We're going to get in so much trouble with Mum and Spencer.' Mo looked more alarmed than he had when he thought Lorelai was going to open the van door.

'It'll be fine,' I said. 'Do you have your phone? We'll use Google maps and hike home. If we get thirsty, we can drink from puddles.'

'What about if we get hungry? Will we have to forage for berries?'

'I expect so,' I said. 'It will be like Bear Grylls.'

'We could take some ice cream with us,' Mo said, brightening up a bit.

'But it's drugged with that Kandy stuff! That's why it tastes so good.'

'You're right,' said Mo. 'We really shouldn't eat it.'

'OMG – I've always wanted to use the squirty ice cream machine!'

'We need to stay low and quiet,' Mo said. 'Or he'll hear us.'

'But look at it, Mo. Look at the buttons, and the shiny lever. And look at that tube where the ice cream comes out. You could stand underneath with your mouth open while I swirl it in. We could take turns!'

'OK, but we need to be ready to run.'

'Of course! Pull a box over that we can stand on – it's too high to reach.'

Mo dragged a box across the floor of the van, just as we drove over a bump. Whatever was in the box made a metallic clanging sound.

'The armband!' Mo said and lifted the flap of the box.

The armband wasn't inside, but there were lots of random metal things: keys, jewellery, coins – stuff like that.

'It's like when you go through security at the airport,' I said. 'And you have to walk into that metal detecting machine. I wonder why these are here?'

The van suddenly jerked to a stop.

'Quick!' Mo said, grabbing for the door handle. He yanked it down and the door opened. The beautiful world was right there in front of us – I could almost taste the freedom. 'You go first!' I climbed out of the van, just as it started to move forwards.

'Jump, Mo!' I shouted.

I didn't think he'd do it, but he did. He leapt like a little orange capybara, scraping his knee as he rolled onto the floor. As the van drove off with the door still open, we crawled behind a parked car and hid, trying to catch our breath.

'We're only two roads away from home,' Mo said. 'Why did he stop?'

'That's the power of the lollipop,' a familiar voice said. Two large feet appeared around the side of the car, along with a neon yellow coat and a sellotaped stick.

Hector was standing in front of us.

Hector

Mo

'Did you stop Mr Gideon's van?' I said, looking up at Hector and trying to ignore the blood trickling down my knee.

'I did,' Hector said.

'But there's no crossing.'

'When you wield an instrument as mighty as this one, you can make crossings wherever you go. All you have to do is stand in the middle of the road and bang it on the ground. People stop – most of the time. I think mine is broken though: it doesn't always work properly.'

'Of course it's broken; it's being held together by sellotape,' Lottie said.

'I meant it's broken internally – it only functions intermittently.'

'Hold on,' I said. 'It's a stick. What do you think it's supposed to do?'

'Stop traffic. Obviously.' Hector rolled his eyes.

'But how exactly do you think it does that?'

'You point it at the vehicles and it controls their braking systems, forcing them to stop.'

'What?' Lottie snorted.

'Wait, let me get this straight,' I stood up with difficulty – my knee was starting to sting. 'Are you saying that you think there is technology inside the lollipop that is so advanced it can control any approaching vehicle, just by waving the stick around?'

'Is that not right?' Hector frowned.

Lottie and me looked at each other and burst out laughing.

'What?' Hector looked confused. 'What does it do, then?'

After the terrifying ten minutes we'd just been through, the look on Hector's face was just incredibly funny. We laughed *so* hard.

'Hey!' Hector said. 'This is a bit harsh. I'm not from these parts – how am I supposed to know? How does it work then? I know you're dying to tell me.'

'Well, you stand in the road…' Lottie said.

'…and hold the stick…' I added.

'…and hope for the best.'

Hector's face fell and we started laughing again.

'What?' He looked panicked. 'You mean they aren't forced to stop? I have no control? So I'm risking my life every time I step off the pavement?'

'Yep,' said Lottie.

'The cars could just run you over if they wanted to,' I said.

'You could get flattened.' Lottie patted his arm.

'You could get squished.' I nodded.

'Sorry.' Lottie and me looked at each other. 'Not sorry!'

'I'm glad you find it so funny. Where I come from, we don't have lollipop people. It's all tech. Crossings are sensor activated.'

'Where do you come from?' I asked.

'I'd have thought you would have worked that out by now,' Hector said. 'I come from the future.'

Lottie's face looms close to the camera

Lottie:
Dun, dun, duuuuuuuuun.

Mo:
What are you doing?

Lottie:

Dramatic sound effects, obviously.

Mo:

Why?

Lottie:

To demonstrate to the viewers how important this moment of the story is.

Mo:

I think they can work that out for themselves. You know, with the mental lollipop man saying he's from the future. The 'dun dun duuuuuun' was implied.

Lottie:

Being subtle never got anybody anywhere, Mo.

Mo:

How would you know? You've never been subtle in your life.

Lottie:

Life is so much simpler if people come right out with stuff.

Mo:
Sometimes it's better to let people work things out for themselves.

Lottie *whispers loudly*:
Do you think they've worked it out, yet?

Mo:
I've told you before: there's no point whispering if your whispering voice is louder than your normal voice.

Lottie *whispers slightly more quietly but still loud enough for the microphone to pick up every word*:
I was pretend whispering, to give the listeners a clue but, at the same time, make them think I was trying to hide the clue. You see – I can be super-subtle!

Mo:
Seeing as they just heard all of that, I'm sticking with my original statement that you're not.

Mo
'You're not a Junker, though,' I said.

'How do you know that, Mo?' Lottie shouted. 'He's crazy; he's been watching us for weeks; and he has strawberry laces falling out of his pocket.'

'Not mouse brains,' I sniggered.

'What's this about mouse brains?' Hector said.

'Your pocket,' said Lottie, 'is full of sweets.'

Hector looked down at the squiggly red lace worming its way out of his pocket. He pulled it out and crammed it into his mouth.

'Well spotted,' he said. 'Yes, Junkers do eat a lot of sugar, but so does anyone who comes back from the future. Friends included.'

'You're the one who left us the envelope,' I said. 'I figured it wasn't Mr Gideon when we found out he's Lorelai's boyfriend.'

'Gideon Melville is Lorelai's husband, actually,' Hector said between chews. 'And Jax is their son.' He picked a bit of lace from between his teeth, examined it on the end of his finger and then put it back into his mouth and swallowed. 'Don't judge me.'

'How do we know we can trust you?' Lottie said. She'd never liked Hector and she hated being proved wrong.

'I just rescued you from a Junker's ice cream van.'

'Excuse me,' Lottie said, 'You only stopped the van. We actually rescued ourselves.'

'We couldn't have got out without his help, Lottie,' I said.

'And I've been giving you warnings, and information to help you,' Hector pointed out.

'He did, Lottie – his information helped us a lot.'

'We worked most of it out for ourselves,' Lottie said.

'Yeah, all by ourselves, we randomly worked out that there are people called Junkers who abduct children and can time-jump,' I said. She was being ridiculously stubborn.

'Maybe not that, specifically,' she said. 'But we worked out other stuff.'

'Look,' said Hector. 'I'm a friend from the future. When we found out you might be being hunted by the Junkers, I was sent back in time to help you.'

'Who sent you?' I said.

'You did. Both of you.'

'You know future us?' Lottie said.

'I know you both very well. We're like family.'

Lottie and me looked at each other, and then a

hundred questions exploded out of both of our mouths.

'What's my hair like in the future?' Lottie said.

'Am I a professor?' I said.

'Have I climbed Mount Everest single-handedly?' said Lottie. 'And do I have a pet gorilla?'

'Have I successfully trained an army of ants?' There were so many things I wanted to know!

'I'll tell you one thing,' Hector said, 'the bossy and annoying stuff you do doesn't ever change.'

'Excellent,' said Lottie.

'But you guys have watched all the time-travel movies,' Hector said. 'You know how this works. I can't mess with the timeline. I can't tell you anything that might change the future.'

'But you already told us a whole bunch of stuff,' I said.

'Ah, yes. Maybe one or two things. But you two didn't seem to understand the danger you were in. You weren't taking it seriously at all. And if you should fail, or if anything bad happens to you, then we're all doomed.'

'Listen, Hector, if that even is your real name,' Lottie said. 'You chose to send us creepy notes and nutty envelopes full of forbidden information. We didn't make you. Don't blame it on us.'

'Calm down, Lott-Lott. I come in peace.' Hector stuck his fingers up at us.

'What?' Lottie said.

'Peace. You know – I believe this is the gesture you use to symbolize peace?' He pointed at his swearing fingers with his other hand.

'Hector,' I said. 'You're giving us the two-finger swear.'

'Really? This is a swear? How have I got that wrong?'

'You have to turn your hand the other way to say peace,' Lottie said. 'Everyone knows that.'

'But why would you make the peace sign and the two-finger swear sign so similar?' Hector frowned. 'That's just asking for trouble.'

'And you need to hold them still, not wiggle them,' I said.

'Yeah, now you're doing bunny ears,' Lottie rolled her eyes. 'You shouldn't really do that to someone unless they're your friend.'

'Otherwise it can come across as a bit mean,' I said. 'Like you're making fun of them.'

'Bunny ears?' Hector looked very confused.

'Yes,' Lottie was getting seriously annoyed. 'You know – you photo bomb. You do the bunny ears.'

'Why do you have all these ridiculous hand gestures? How completely stupid!' Hector made a face and put his hand in his pocket.

'I can show you some other hand gestures if you like,' Lottie said.

We were getting nowhere.

'Shall we just all agree to be friends and move forwards?' I said. 'We've got quite a lot on and, if we don't get home soon, Mum's going to notice we're gone and then we really will be doomed. Also, I'm a little bit worried about Mr Gideon coming back and finding us and abducting us for real.'

'Good point, Mo. Quite right,' Hector said.

'Fine,' said Lottie. 'So what happens next?'

'We need to talk,' said Hector. 'And you two need to work on that competition entry. Don't want to pile the pressure on, but...'

'Yes, we know,' I said. 'We have to win.'

Squirrel Attack

Mo

We needed to talk to Hector, but we were out of time, so there was only one option.

'You're going to have to come over,' I said.

'Now?'

'Yes. And we're also going to have to explain my knee, which really hurts by the way – thanks for asking, everyone.'

'I have a genius plan,' Lottie said. 'Everybody follow me!'

We walked home as sneakily as we could, ducking behind trees and parked cars. When we reached our stretch of the road, we stopped for a second to make sure nobody was watching from the windows, and then raced up the steps to our front door. I was a bit concerned about Lottie's plan, but I had no ideas myself, and it was an emergency situation.

She opened the door and yelled, 'Emma, come quick!'

I heard a chair scrape and bang and Mum

came running out of the kitchen towards us, looking alarmed. 'Mo, you're bleeding!' she said, scooping me up like a toddler and carrying me into the bathroom. 'What happened?' She looked at Hector. 'And I don't mean to be rude, but...'

'This is Hector. He's the lollipop man from school,' Lottie said. 'And a brilliant job he does, too.' She winked.

'Lovely to meet you,' Mum glanced at Hector while examining my knee.

'So lovely to meet you,' Hector smiled at Mum in a very strange way.

'Let me explain what happened,' Lottie said. 'Mo thought he heard a noise outside, so he leapt like a graceful gazelle... [she demonstrated the leap] over to the window to check it out. "Hector's in trouble!" he said, as he ran heroically out of the front door and down the steps to where Hector was being attacked by a raging squirrel. I've never seen anything like it before – all teeth and claws...' She did an impression of a wild animal slashing and biting, then she paused dramatically and looked around at us all. 'Mo fought off the squirrel and fell, scraping his knee, which resulted in the injury you see before you.'

'Gosh,' said Mum. 'A raging squirrel?' She looked at me.

'It was extra ragey,' I said.

'I don't know what I would have done if Mo hadn't seen me being attacked as I happened to be walking past your house,' said Hector.

'You'd probably be dead. Ripped to shreds. Nothing left but bloody little pieces on the ground for the birds to peck at.' Lottie was taking it too far, as always.

'And you work at the school?' Mum looked up at Hector.

'Yes. My job is to protect your children, which I have been doing to the best of my ability.'

'What happened to Derek?' Mum asked.

'He left to be with his own kind,' Lottie said. 'In a special retirement home for lollipop men.'

Hector smiled at Mum again. 'It really is awfully nice to meet you.'

Mum looked at him for a moment, and I saw the worry on her face fall away as it melted into a smile. I think she saw what I saw whenever I looked at Hector – there was just something about him that I liked.

'Well, thank you for returning my brave Mo-Bear,' she said. 'Let me get him cleaned up and then I'll make us all a cup of tea.'

Lottie

I noticed that nobody congratulated me on my quick thinking and incredible re-enactment, but I was too busy watching the weirdness going on between Emma and Hector to tell them off.

When we were sat in the living room and Emma went to the kitchen, I turned to him. 'Why are you flirting with Emma?'

'I am most definitely not flirting with Emma,' Hector said.

'But you're looking at her like she's your favourite celebrity crush.'

'I like her,' Hector said. 'She's kind and she smells like pancakes and strawberries.'

'Well, hands off,' I said. 'My dad has already dibsed her.'

I didn't know why it bothered me so much, but it put me in rather a bad mood.

'We don't have time to talk about this now,' said Mo. 'We only have a few minutes and there are more important things to discuss.'

I knew he was right, so I settled for giving Hector the stink-eye.

'So, I guess you guys have more questions.' Hector was sitting on the sofa, still wearing his lollipop man coat with his hat pulled low.

'Ooh!' I said, putting my hand up.

'Yes!' said Mo, jumping out of his chair.

'And by questions, I mean questions about the predicament you are in and not about irrelevant stuff from the future.'

I put my hand in my lap, feeling extremely disappointed, and Mo sat back down.

'Can you tell us more about why the Junkers are after us?' Mo asked.

'I can tell you a bit, but there's only so much I can say without it having a dangerous effect on the future,' Hector said. 'You see, everything we do and say, no matter how small, creates ripples which...'

'Yeah, yeah,' I said. 'We've all seen *Doctor Who*. We know about spoilers and rips in the fabric of the space-time continuum, or whatever.'

'Just tell us what you can, please,' said Mo.

'OK. I guess I should start with the Discovery Competition. You guys have to win.'

'You already told us that!' I was getting impatient. 'Why do we have to win?'

Sadie came into the room and sat next to Hector. He sort of chuckled when he saw her, although I couldn't think what he had found amusing.

'It's fine to talk in front of Sadie,' I said. 'She's part of the team.'

'The work you've done for the Discovery Competition,' Hector said, looking at Mo, 'will one day put the Junkers out of business. You're going to change the world.'

'What? Mo is?' I said.

'Oh yes, he wins awards and everything.'

'Mo does?'

'Yes.'

'This Mo.'

'The Mo sitting in front of me now.'

'Are you sure?'

'I'm certain.'

'It seems unlikely.'

'Hey, I'm standing right here!' Mo stood up and flapped his arms about.

'I'm just saying what everyone else is thinking,' I said.

'I'm sure nobody else is thinking that, Lottie,' Hector frowned. 'You should have a bit more faith in your brother.'

'Nonsense,' I said. 'Sadie was thinking it, weren't you, Sadie?'

'Purrow meowt.'

'Now, Sadie,' Hector said, 'that's just plain rude.'

'What did she say?' Mo was still flapping.

'Probably best I don't repeat it, to be honest, Mo.' Hector made a face.

'Hang on,' Mo said. 'How can you understand her?'

Hector's eyes went wide for a second, and then he said, 'In the future, the most commonly spoken language is Cattish.'

'Really?' Mo was sucking it up, just because he was Hector's favourite.

'Sure,' said Hector. 'Maybe.'

'So anyway, Mo is going to invent something, blahdy blahdy blah,' I said. 'That doesn't explain why they're after me, too.'

'Ah, yes,' Hector said. 'He can't do it without your help.'

'Obviously.' I rolled my eyes.

'And I suspect the Junkers can only take one of

you, so they're probably deciding which of you to junk.'

'Why can they only take one of us?' Mo said.

'It's complicated,' Hector sighed. 'But to simplify: it's to do with the power required for time-jumping. It's easy to jump from the future to the past. Jumping requires a huge surge of power, and in the future we have power sources strong enough to provide that surge. In this time, there simply isn't enough power.'

'So how do you power a time-jump?' I asked.

'To make a jump from this time, we have to use the sun as a power source.'

'Solar flares!' Mo said.

'Exactly,' said Hector. 'An X-class solar flare provides enough power, momentarily, for a single jump. But the Junkers need to make two jumps: one to send the – erm – junkee to the Junkyard, and the other to allow them to escape back into the future soon afterwards, before the disappearance of the junkee is investigated.'

'And two X-class solar flares occurring close together is quite rare!' Mo was getting very over-excited about all the sciency stuff.

'So they come back and wait to make their move, just before a double flare.'

'What's with all the parts in their house, then?' I said. 'What are they building?'

'That I don't know,' Hector said.

'Something to take back to the future with them?' Mo peeped out of the window at the Junker house opposite.

'It can't be that – it's impossible to time-jump with any sort of metal on you. It would cause an explosion.'

'That makes sense,' I said. 'In books and stuff people quite often have to time travel wearing just their pants.'

'So, if the Junkers were to junk someone who had a watch on, for example,' said Mo, 'it would blow all of them up?'

'Ooh.' I jumped up. 'That's why Mr Gideon had that box of metal stuff in his van – he must have taken it from people before he junked them!'

'Lottie, you're right!' Mo said. Of course I was.

'Here we are,' Emma walked into the room carrying a tray of tea and biscuits. 'How's your knee, Mo-Bear?'

'It hurts a bit,' he sniffed.

'At least you both seem to be over that food

poisoning now,' Emma smiled. 'You need to build your strength back up.'

Mo, Sadie and I stuffed ourselves with biscuits while Emma and Hector chatted, with him giving her that goofy smile the whole time.

'Hector,' Emma said. 'I do love that name.'

Hector stayed for a while, drinking tea with six sugars, and stroking Schrody who sat on his lap. We didn't get another chance to speak to him alone. I had been quite hard on him but, after spending that time together, I did believe we could trust him. After he left, Mo, Sadie, Schrody and I went up to Mo's room. We had a lot to think about.

'If only we could have asked him some more questions,' Mo said. 'There's still so much we don't know.'

'Why don't we write a list?' I said. 'We could pass a note to him when we cross the road tomorrow, and he could pass us one back on the way home. Assuming, of course, that he hasn't been fired.'

'That's actually a good idea,' said Mo.

'Why do you always seem so surprised when I have a good idea?' I asked. 'It's insulting.'

I thought he'd argue, but he just thought for a moment, and said, 'Sorry, Lottie. I'm not used to working with other people. I've always thought that I was glad to be alone because I'm smarter than everyone else and they'd only mess things up. It's hard, now, getting used to the idea that I was wrong to think that. You're just as smart as me and it's much better being part of a team.'

'What?' I said. Surely he was winding me up.

'I said I'm sorry.'

'If you think I'm an idiot, you should just come out and say it.'

'I don't though.'

I felt furious. 'Whatever, Mo. Let's write the list.'

You'll find it in the evidence box, labelled Exhibit S.

Questions for Hector

How does time travel work?

What does a time machine look like?

How does junking work?

Does it use the same equipment as a time machine?

'We'll give this to him on our way to school tomorrow morning,' I said, 'And hopefully he'll be able to answer us at home time.'

'I don't know how much he'll be able to tell us. You know, without potentially destroying the future for everyone on Earth.'

'You need to chill, Mo. It'll be fine.'

'What if we're being watched, though?'

'Who would be watching us?'

'I don't know – the Discovery Competition judges; the Time-Jump Spoiler Police; the Junkers. I don't want it to look like we're cheating. I don't want to get arrested and put in Time-Jump Spoiler jail. And I don't want us, or Hector to get junked.'

'I don't see how anyone would suspect Hector of being capable of any of those things,' I said. 'No offence, but he comes across as a bit of an idiot.'

'That's really mean, Lottie.'

'Weren't you listening? I said "no offence".'

'It doesn't count if you follow it by saying something offensive.'

'Have you got our Discovery invention working yet, Mo?'

I've never been exactly sure what a scowl is, but

if I had to guess, I'd say it was the expression on Mo's face at that moment. He stomped over to his desk and I smiled to myself. My brother was kind of adorable when he was cross.

The Police

Mo

The next morning, I was relieved to see Hector waiting at the crossing as usual. I know Lottie thought I was being silly, but I couldn't help worrying about all the things that could go wrong. We knew the Junkers were watching us all the time – Jax in school; Lorelai from her house – and we were constantly listening out for the tinkling of 'Who's Afraid of the Big Bad Wolf'. We knew that even if we couldn't see Mr Gideon, he was probably lurking around a corner. If the Junkers saw Hector talking to us, they might realise he was our ally and do something nasty to him.

As he stood on the crossing to let us pass, I put my hand up to give him a high-five. He looked a bit confused, but smiled and winked when he high-fived me back and I put our note in his hand.

'Message delivered?' Lottie said, once we reached the other side.

'Affirmative,' I nodded.

Now all we had to do was get through a day of

pretending to be friends with Jax, and then, at 3:30, we should get some answers.

Lottie avoided Jax as much as possible. If we were standing in the playground and she saw him coming, she pulled me away to do something else. But Lottie being Lottie, she couldn't resist spending time with her other friends, catching up on what we'd missed while we were off sick. She couldn't stay by my side every second.

At lunchtime, she finished her baguette in four big bites.

'You're so slow, Mo,' she said. 'Ha! Slow, Mo – like slow-mo – get it?'

'Yep,' I said, picking up a carrot stick.

'Do you mind if I go and talk to Simran and Summer for a bit? Just while you're finishing?'

'Nope,' I said, but she had already run off.

Jax sat down next to me. 'Hey, Mo.'

I felt a bit uncomfortable. 'Oh, hey, Jax.'

'Are you all better now? You were sick, weren't you?' He watched me shovelling lasagna into my mouth.

'Yes, I'm fine, thanks. Just a one-off thing.'

'That's good, then,' he said.

'Yeah.' I had no clue what to say. He was my enemy, apparently.

'I don't expect you were able to work on the Discovery project while you were sick?' he said. 'It's almost the deadline and we haven't properly finished.'

Of course, he still thought I was working on a gigantic lost-property database. And, of course, I was working on something completely different. I hated lying. 'I just chilled, mostly,' I said. 'I guess we're not going to be winning the competition.'

'I guess not,' he said. 'I'm sorry, Mo – I know it was really important to you.'

'Yeah, but stuff happens. There are more important things in life than winning a competition.'

'Like family?' he frowned.

'Yes, exactly. Like family,' I said.

'Do you miss your dad?' This was not a question I'd been expecting him to ask – Jax had never mentioned my dad before.

'I've never known him, so I suppose it would be impossible for me to miss him.'

'But you do anyway?'

'It's more of a feeling like knowing something you need is not where it ought to be. Like being hungry – having an emptiness in your belly that almost hurts, but you know there's no food that will fill it up.'

'You have your mum, though. She's great. And you look so much like your parents – that must be nice.'

'I've never really thought about it,' I said. 'I'm glad you like Mum.' I couldn't understand why he'd be asking me these questions. He was staring at his feet, deep in thought. 'Are you OK?' I said.

He looked up. 'Things at home aren't so good.'

'Do you mean with your parents?'

Jax nodded. 'I lost something. Something important that they need for their jobs. They've been so mad at me and have spent most of their time trying to get a replacement sorted out, but it's taking a lot of time. I thought that if I could find the thing I lost, it would make everything OK.'

'Did you find it?'

'Yeah, I did. But I haven't given it to them yet.'

'Why not?'

'Because I don't know if it would make me feel any better. I don't really like their jobs. They spend loads of time away from home. We move around a lot. Other stuff too.'

'You think if you don't give them the lost thing back, they might change their minds and do something else?'

'I wish that could happen, but I don't think it's possible. They like what they do and they're good at it. I don't think giving it back would change anything. Not really.'

'So, what are you going to do?'

'I don't know, Mo.' He looked me right in the eyes. 'What do you think I should do?'

There he was, standing in front of me and giving me the chance to tell him to stuff his parents and give the lost item to me. I wasn't sure whether he knew that I knew he was talking about the armband, and that his parents were Lorelai and Gideon, or if he was just asking a friend for advice. I thought about his empty room – about how lonely he must be living just across the street with parents who weren't that interested in him, and no friends. I had Mum and Schrodinger, and now Spencer, Lottie and Sadie too. I was lucky. I knew I wasn't supposed to trust him, and that Lottie would be furious with me if she thought I'd helped him, but he just looked so sad.

'You can only do what you feel is right,' I said. 'And if you need a friend, I'm here.'

We had to stop ourselves from running to the school gate at home time, we were so desperate to get to Hector. There were giant holes in the information we had and he was the only person who could fill them in for us. But we didn't want to make anyone suspicious, so we tried our hardest to act casual.

As we walked through the gate, we could see a large crowd gathered at the crossing and could hear the sounds of a struggle.

'Oh no, what's he done now?' Lottie said, as we forgot about acting casual and ran towards the road to see what was going on.

'I haven't done anything wrong!' Hector was shouting, as a policeman stood in front of him, looking frighteningly serious. Another policeman stood a few metres away, talking to a lady in a purple coat with straight brown hair who was crying into a tissue.

'That's as maybe,' the first policeman said. 'But an allegation has been made and we need to bring you in for questioning.'

'But I don't even know who that woman is,' Hector said, glaring at the crying lady.

'What an outrageous lie!' the lady shouted, before sobbing even louder.

'You're the liar,' Hector said.

'Come on, sir,' the first policeman took a step closer to him. 'Let's sort this out at the station.'

'I'm not going. You can't make me.'

'I'm afraid we can if we have to, sir,' the policeman reached for his radio.

'Let me just tie my shoe while we discuss this,' Hector said, kneeling down so that the bottom of his coat spread around his feet like a neon yellow puddle.

'Be quick, please, sir. We need to continue this conversation at the station.'

'But there's no evidence! I've been framed, guv'nor! It's all circumstantial! Call in forensics if you don't believe me!'

'Sir, none of those comments bear any relevance to the request we've issued you.'

'Why's he shouting random phrases from cop shows?' I said. 'I don't think that's going to help.'

'He's nuts,' Lottie said.

'If you were to investigate the scene,' Hector

continued, 'and get your CSIs to examine the clues, they'll understand exactly what I mean.'

'Come on, sir, let's not make a fuss in front of the kids.'

'But the answer is right under your noses,' Hector looked over at us. '*Underneath your feet.*'

The policemen moved to either side of him and firmly held his arms. The crying lady had gone.

'I see there are *two* of you. Do you have two cars? Two separate modes of transportation?'

'No, sir, just the one car. We're taking you to it right now.' The policemen led him away down the street to where a car was waiting.

Hector glanced around at us one last time and wiggled his eyebrows.

We watched in silence as he got in the car and was driven away, then waited while the crowds gradually disappeared on their journeys home.

'Why has he been arrested?' I said. 'He would never hurt anyone.'

'I know, Mo. He might be weird but he's not a criminal.'

'Why would that lady make things up about him?'

'Didn't you notice anything familiar about her? Or her hair?'

There had been something pulling at my memory when I looked at the lady, but I couldn't make it stick. 'What about her hair?'

'We've seen it before, Mo. But not on that woman's head. Remember what the Junker poem said – they're masters of disguise.'

A feeling of horror seeped through me. 'It was Lorelai.'

'It was Lorelai,' Lottie nodded. 'She must have seen Hector with us and decided to get him out of the way.'

'Poor Hector,' I said. 'It seemed like he was trying to tell us something.'

'How did you make that out? I thought he was just talking nonsense like usual,' Lottie frowned.

'All that stuff about evidence underneath our feet – he was looking right at us.'

We both looked down.

On the middle white stripe of the zebra crossing, I could see a small squiggly red shape. There were no cars in sight, so I pulled Lottie into the middle of the road and pointed.

'What is that?' she said.

It was a bunch of strawberry laces placed into the shape of a square within a square.

'I've seen it before.'

'On the metal armband thingy!' Lottie gasped.

'Hector must have made it when he tied his shoe!'

'That was actually quite clever of him.'

'It was,' I agreed. 'We have to work out why he left it and what it means.'

As we looked down at the strawberry cube, a familiar sound crept into my ears. It was faint at first so I didn't really think about it until Lottie started singing: 'Who's afraid of the big bad wolf, the big bad wolf, the big bad wolf...'

'Shush a sec,' I said, grabbing her elbow.

The music was getting louder.

'Mr Gideon's coming!' I said.

'Ooh, ice cream!' Lottie clapped her hands.

'Yes,' I said, feeling around in my pocket for coins. 'Wait – no! He's a Junker, Lottie; we can't let him find us here alone.'

'But...'

'I know, I want ice cream, too. But he's evil, and the ice cream is full of Kandy, remember?'

'Yes,' she said, looking a bit confused.

'And we found that box in his van, of things he took from the people he junked.'

'Yes,' she said, her eyes wide. 'We need to get rid of this diagram. We don't want him to know we know!'

We both started kicking at the strawberry laces, trying to destroy the picture. It was harder than you might think because they were sort of stuck to the ground. In the end we bent down and scraped them off with our fingernails, until there were just a few broken red worms on the white stripe.

'I can see him – he's almost here!' Lottie panted, pulling my sleeve. 'We have to go, Mo!'

We ran.

Lottie

We ran so fast I thought my lungs were going to explode. We leapt up the steps to our house, two at a time, opened the door, and slammed it behind us. Then we sank to the floor, trying to catch our breath.

'Have you two been racing again?' Emma said, hanging up our school bags.

'Yes,' I panted. 'I won.'

'Only because I'm injured,' Mo said, holding the knee he'd scraped jumping out of Mr Gideon's van.

'OMG, Mo, will you ever stop going on about that tiny little cut?' I said.

'Shut up, Lottie. I think it's bleeding again.' He rolled up his trouser leg: there was a bit of blood oozing through the plaster.

'I'd better have another look at that,' Emma said.

'Let me rip the plaster off for you!' I leant over it and reached for one of the corners.

'Get off, Lottie – I'll do it!'

'It's better this way,' I said. 'I'll be quick. It won't even hurt.'

'It will. You won't be gentle.'

'Fine,' I said. 'There's a spider behind you, just FYI.' As Mo turned in alarm, I ripped the plaster off hard and fast.

'Ow!' Mo said. 'I hate you!'

'That looks like a nasty wound,' said a voice that gave me the chills. 'How did it happen?'

Lorelai was standing in our hallway wearing a purple coat and looking slightly out of breath.

'My Mo-Bear fell while rescuing the school lollipop man from a rampaging squirrel,' Emma said, pulling Mo up while we both just stared at her.

'What a brave boy,' Lorelai said. 'I hope Hector was grateful.'

'He was lovely, actually,' Emma said. 'Are you off now, Lorelai? That was a quick visit.'

'Yes, I'll let you see to your boy,' she smiled at me and Mo, but it wasn't a friendly smile. 'See you soon, lovely lady! And look after these adorable children of yours. We wouldn't want them having any more accidents, would we?'

My heart only started beating again as the door closed behind her.

'What was she doing here?' I asked Sadie, while Emma was re-plastering Mo's knee.

'Merow merow mew,' Sadie said.

'Nosey cow,' I said. 'She's trying to find out what we've invented for the Discovery Competition. I hate the way she sucks up to Emma, just so she can get information.'

'Meow.'

'Yes, we'd better tell Mo not to tell Emma too much about what we're doing. If she doesn't know, she can't tell Lorelai, can she?'

'Perew mew meowl?'

'I know Emma's super-nice, Sadie, but I still don't think she'll believe us if we try to explain what's going on. And Dad definitely won't. We need a team meeting upstairs. Go and get Mo.'

Sadie saluted and walked towards the kitchen.

'And tell him to bring cheese slices!' I called after her.

Flares

Lottie

'We need to recap everything we know,' I said, when Mo walked into the room with a plate of cheese on toast. 'I said cheese slices! Why can't anyone around here follow simple instructions?'

'I don't understand Sadie, remember?' Mo huffed. 'And you could always go and get your cheese slices yourself.'

'Cheese on toast will have to do,' I said as Schrody dragged a slice off the plate and started licking it.

'I'm closing the curtains,' Mo said, shuffling on his bottom over to the window with a piece of cheesy toast hanging out of his mouth. 'The Junkers seem to be watching us wherever we go, I wouldn't be surprised if they have a telescope set up so they can spy on us through the windows.'

'I was going to suggest that myself,' I said. 'From now on, everything we do must be kept completely secret. We'll only talk openly about the competition, Hector and the Junkers when we are in this room with the door shut and the curtains closed.'

'Stealth mode,' Mo nodded.

'So: the Junkers know about Hector.'

'And got him arrested,' Mo said. 'They must have known he was helping us and wanted to get rid of him.'

'But if the Junkers wanted to make him disappear,' I said, 'Why not just junk him?'

'They can't, remember? They need to wait for a Class X solar flare.'

'Oh yes, the solar flares. If we knew when they were going to be, we'd have a much better idea of when we'll be in the most danger.'

'But we can't possibly know when a flare is going to happen.'

'The list!' I gasped. 'The one Sadie stole from Lorelai! Didn't that say something about occurring Xs?'

'It had dates from the past and the future!' Mo said. 'You're right, Lottie.'

'But we don't have it – I told Sadie to throw it away. I thought it was worthless. What did you do with it, Sadie?'

Sadie just shrugged.

Mo jumped up and ran to his bed. 'I keep telling you, Lottie. Nothing is worthless. Everything is valuable to someone. That's why I keep the things I find.'

He rummaged around in his secret box and pulled out a folded-up piece of paper.

'How?' I asked, bobbing up and down with excitement.

'Sadie dropped it. I found it and I couldn't throw it away.'

'Oh, Mo – you wonderful, awesome, weird little hoarder – I love you!' I hugged him. Usually, he stands there awkwardly when anybody touches him, his arms down by his sides and his back all stiff. But this time he actually hugged me back.

We unfolded the paper and put it on the floor in front of us. You can find it in the box, labelled Exhibit N.

Class X Occurrences 2000-2020

Year	Month	Date	Time of Peak	Class
2000	December	8th	15:45	X 3.12
2001	April	9th	06:28	X 1.87
2001	July	30th	00:18	X 24.51
2002	March	26th	22:43	X 6.82
2002	November	12th	23:22	X 19.22
2003	February	27th	17:09	X 8.64
2003	December	15th	12:36	50.6938N
2004	October	18th	02:01	X 29.55
2005	March	3rd	00:56	X 6.85
2005	April	14th	13:16	X 1.21
2005	July	9th	14:53	X 5.98
2006	July	26th	09:55	X 28.66
2007	January	8th	10:52	X 13.11
2007	May	22nd	08:30	X 7.72
2007	June	21st	18:07	X 9.12
2008	**August**	**5th**	**15:12**	**X 5.78**
2008	**August**	**5th**	**16:09**	**X 6.21**
2009	February	1st	16:42	X 11.12
2009	June	19th	07:47	X 18.65
2009	December	26th	07:15	1.3047W
2010	May	12th	21:28	X 4.42
2011	March	4th	20:04	X 8.99
2012	September	18th	21:24	X 12.53
2013	April	29th	17:19	X 17.12
2013	April	30th	11:33	X 3.32
2014	November	18th	09:19	X 1.18
2015	May	5th	22:41	X 1.43
2016	July	26th	08:23	X 1.98
2016	November	11th	10:00	X 2.66
2017	February	5th	00:52	X 12.65
2017	February	20th	04:40	X 17.88
2017	May	20th	14:37	X 1.99
2018	April	6th	03:13	X 22.98
2018	**October**	**31st**	**18:42**	**X 4.56**
2018	**October**	**31st**	**20:56**	**X 3.87**
2019	February	10th	03:47	X 9.91
2019	**June**	**28th**	**15:05**	**X 6.59**
2019	**June**	**28th**	**16:04**	**X 7.29**
2020	September	9th	22:22	X 15.39

'This is brilliant,' Mo said. 'We can see when they're likely to make their move.' He pointed at a place on the list. 'Look – on the 31st of October there are going to be two powerful flares, at 6:42pm and then at 8.56pm. That will be it! That's the date they're waiting for!'

'Halloween,' I said, feeling excited. 'That's a great day to be doing something evil.'

'Don't look so happy about it, Lottie. The evil thing they're going to be doing is abducting one of us and sending us to a scary place that we can never come back from.'

'I know, but you have to appreciate the timing.'

'So, we know when it's going to happen,' Mo said. 'What we don't know is exactly how it's going to happen.'

'And that takes us back to Hector and his clues…'

'The cube thing he drew,' Mo said, walking over to his desk and opening his laptop. 'I've seen it before, and not just on the armband.'

'The questions we asked Hector were all about time-jumping and junking,' I said. 'So it must have something to do with that.'

'Did you notice he also said a load of stuff

about two separate cars?' Mo didn't look up from Google. 'It seemed a bit weird at the time, but I think it was another clue. Remember we asked him if the time-jumping and junking was done the same way? I think that was his way of telling us that they involve separate ways of travelling.'

'You worked that out from his crazy ramblings?' I said. 'It's really lucky that you speak nerd.'

'And I think I've found out what the mystery cube thing is.'

'What is it?'

'It's a tesseract.'

'That means absolutely nothing to me,' I said, disappointed.

'It's a four-dimensional hypercube.'

'Still nothing.'

'It's really complicated,' Mo said. 'But I think it must have something to do with how the time-jumping works. How fascinating.'

He started clicking away on his laptop. I waited for at least twenty minutes while he read through pages of stuff, the silence broken only by mousepad clicks and his 'oohs' and 'ahs'. I have to tell you, it was very boring. He tried to explain some of it to me, but it was all geometry and maths and, to be honest with you, none of it really mattered to me at that point.

'Yes, extremely fascinating,' I said. 'But the important thing right now is to work out what it means to us.'

'It means time travel is possible, Lottie. I don't know exactly how, but just the idea of it is mind blowing!'

'Mo,' I said, pulling the laptop away from him and closing the lid. 'Focus! The only thing we need to understand is how we can use this information to help us. Halloween is next week. Evil people are going to try to junk one of us – probably me...' (Mo rolled his eyes.) 'And we need to make sure that doesn't happen. Not just for ourselves but for the good of the world and the future and the human race.'

'Right,' said Mo. 'Sorry.'

'The tessa-square is on that armband that Jax stole from us. He also drew it on the competition poster. We know it's important.'

'I think the armband is one of the time-jumping devices.'

'You think the time-machine is a bracelet? How

would that work? You put it on and it zaps you through space?'

'It could only work for one person,' Mo said. 'And the Junkers left it behind, remember? They went back to the future without it.'

'So it must be the junking device,' I said. 'The main time machine that they use to transport all of them backwards and forwards is something else.'

'Something we haven't seen yet. Something that can transport more than one person at a time.'

'But that means we had our hands on the junking bracelet and we let Jax steal it!' How terribly upsetting. 'If we'd known it was that important, we could have stashed it in Gringott's instead of in a cardboard box under your bed.'

'It was a secret box, Lottie.'

'Like that would make a difference to anyone except you.'

'What's that supposed to mean?' Mo looked annoyed.

'It means that everybody in this house has looked in everybody else's secret boxes.'

'What?'

'You're the only person who respects the secrecy rule, Mo.'

'You mean you've looked in my box?' His cheeks were red.

'Of course! I've looked in your box, Sadie's box, Dad's box and Emma's box. What on earth did you expect?'

'Oh, I don't know… FOR MY PRIVACY TO BE RESPECTED!'

'We're going off topic again,' I said. 'Do you think we should have another go at breaking into the Junker house to see if we can find the junking bracelet?'

'It's a big risk, Lottie. It went pretty badly last time,' Mo said. 'And we looked everywhere but didn't find it.'

'I suppose,' I said. 'I'm happy to put myself through terrible danger, but only for good reason.'

'I say we avoid going to that house unless we absolutely, one hundred per cent, have to.'

'Agreed,' I said. 'So we only have one other option and, I'm afraid, you're not going to like it.'

Things Get Dark

Mo

I couldn't believe what she was suggesting.

'No, Lottie. We are not torturing Jax.'

'Let's think it through first, before we make a decision,' Lottie said, in an annoying way, as if she was talking to a baby or a really, really old person.

'I've thought it through. It's INSANE!'

'He's the only one of the Junkers we have a chance of overpowering. We don't have to really hurt him, just tie him up and threaten him until he gives us some answers.'

'That's horrible, Lottie. I won't do it.'

'You don't still think he's your friend, do you?'

I kind of did, actually. No matter what had happened between us, I couldn't help thinking that he wanted to be my friend. We had lots in common and he'd always seemed happy when we'd been together.

'Not my friend, exactly, but I think he's a good guy, deep down.'

'He's such a good guy that he pretended to like you so he could sneak into your room, go into your stupid secret box and *steal* from you. Friends don't do that. Good guys don't do that.'

'It's not as simple as that, Lottie.'

'Seems pretty simple to me.'

'Well, if that's the way you want to look at things, would you call someone who snooped through your private things a friend?'

'It was for your own good,' Lottie said. 'If I hadn't taken a look inside everyone's secret boxes, I wouldn't know half the useful stuff I do.'

'It's still wrong.'

'Don't you want to know what your mum has in her box? Here's a spoiler – it's all stuff to do with your dad.'

What? Everything stopped for a moment. I didn't know my mum had kept Dad's stuff, or why she hadn't told me about it, but I felt hurt. He was my dad. Surely it was my right to see? I felt tears prickle the backs of my eyes.

'She's probably keeping it to show to you when you're older,' Lottie said gently, looking as though she felt bad. 'You know what grown-ups are like – they always think we won't be able to handle anything, when actually we're far better at handling things than they are.'

I nodded. I knew Mum would never mean to hurt me. And I knew it was wrong to look through people's private things. But I was desperate to see.

'I know where the box is,' Lottie said. 'What if I were to go and get it, for my own personal benefit, and just look through it while you happen to be here in the room?'

'OK,' I said.

A minute later she came back, with the box. We sat on my bed and she opened it. There wasn't much inside – just a few random things. But they were my dad's things and that made them special. There was a grey hoody, a bit bobbly and faded, folded carefully in the corner. I didn't dare unfold it, in case I couldn't get it back the way it was, but I leant in and sniffed it. I don't know why I thought it would still smell of him – he hadn't worn it for over ten years and the scent would have faded away long ago. It would have been nice, to smell his smell.

There was a glass trophy for contributions to

biomedical science and a cuddly toy – a ginger cat – tucked next to the hoody.

'It looks just like Schrodinger,' Lottie said. 'Let's see if there's anything in the box that might give us a clue.' She started carefully picking things up and inspecting them.

'Look, Mo – this must be your dad,' she said, showing me a photo of Mum and Dad laughing together.

'Yes, that's him,' I said. Mum had given me a few pictures of him so I recognised him straight away.

'Oh, he had a tattoo,' Lottie said, 'How unexpected. I didn't think science geeks had tattoos.'

'I didn't know he had one.' I looked at the photo of my dad, smiling in the sunshine, his T-shirt showing off a tattoo on his right arm. He looked so happy.

I felt a tear roll down my cheek. I suddenly realised why Mum had kept this stuff hidden away. Losing my dad must have been the worst thing that had ever happened to her and looking at his stuff could only make her feel that pain all over again. This box was private and it felt wrong to be looking through it, even if he was my dad. I knew she'd show me it when she felt ready.

'Let's put it back, Lottie,' I said.

'Are you sure?'

I took one last look as I nodded. 'Wait,' I said. 'What's this?' I picked up a see-through plastic bag that had a label on the front which said 'Metropolitan Police – Recovered Items.'

'It must have been your dad's stuff that they found when he disappeared,' Lottie said, peering through the plastic.

There were keys, coins and something else: a Mr Gideon's Rainbow Swirl lolly wrapper.

I stared at it.

Lottie gasped.

'I've never seen another ice cream van called Mr Gideon's,' I said.

'I don't think there is another one,' Lottie whispered.

'You don't think…' I could hardly bear to think it, let alone say it.

Lottie and me looked at each other for a moment and I knew what had to be done.

'We need to talk to Jax.'

I couldn't sleep that night. I didn't even really try. I thought about my dad: the way he'd disappeared so suddenly and without a trace. The ice cream wrapper could just be a coincidence, but I didn't think so. I wanted to ask Mum, but I knew it would make her sad. She'd seemed so much happier since we moved in with the Buttons and I didn't want anything to ruin that for her.

Dad was a scientist: a biomedical engineer. And his name was Morris, like mine. He was working on building incredible prosthetic body parts, so that if people had an accident and lost an arm, or if their kidney or a section of their heart wasn't working, he could make them a replacement. Had the Junkers taken him to stop me from being born? Or did they take him because his prosthetics meant people wouldn't need to buy their harvested body parts?

I got up and peeped through a gap in the curtains. All the lights in the Junker house were on – I supposed they must be working on building a new junking bracelet in time for Halloween. I shivered. I used to love that house, and they'd made it into something I was afraid of.

I sat at my desk and opened my laptop, bracing

myself to do something that I'd always been too scared to do. I Googled 'Morris Delaney disappearance'. There was something I needed to know.

The article I found is in the evidence box, called Exhibit O.

Fears Growing After Shock Disappearance of Scientist

There is growing concern about the welfare of renowned scientist Morris Delaney, who disappeared on 5th August in mysterious circumstances. Mr Delaney left the home he shared with partner Emma Appleby at around 2:45pm, asserting that he was heading to the shops to buy groceries. He was last seen walking down a local street, with no apparent signs of distress or anything to suggest he would not be returning.

Ms Appleby reported him missing at around 21:00 hours the same evening, after he failed to return and made no contact.

Such behaviour is described as 'completely out of character' for bioengineer Mr Delaney, who is responsible for the most pioneering techniques in human transplants in British medical history. The police admit they have 'no leads' in the case.

I pulled my not-at-all-secret box out from under my bed and found the list of solar flares. I knew what I'd find before I found it, and I knew it would make me sick with dread, but it had to be done.

My dad vanished on 5th August 2008, at approximately 3pm. On 5th August 2008, there were two X-class solar flares, at 3:12pm and 4:09pm. It wasn't a coincidence. My dad hadn't disappeared. He'd been junked.

I opened my desk drawer and looked at the photo of him, which I'd borrowed from my mum's box. He hadn't known what was coming. I wondered if he was frightened when they took him. I wondered if he thought of Mum in the last moments. He never even knew he was going to have a son. For the first time ever, my dad seemed like a real person to me, and not just the idea of a person I had never known. I cried and cried.

Drastic Action

Mo

The next day, I went to school determined to do whatever it took to get some information from Jax.

'You look like you mean business,' Lottie said, as we walked to school.

'So?' I said.

'It's a bit scary, that's all. I'm used to fluffy bunny Mo. This grizzly bear Mo will take some getting used to.'

'I thought you wanted me to toughen up,' I said.

'I thought I did, too.'

'Well, make up your mind, Lottie. If you want me to lock Jax in a cupboard and force him to answer our questions, fluffy bunny Mo isn't going to cut it.'

'Are you OK?' she said.

'No. I'm not OK,' I said. 'Everything is horrible and I hate feeling like this.'

'I'm sorry, Mo.' She squeezed my hand.

'Let's just get this done.'

We crossed the road with no Hector to help us, and walked through the school gates.

With the presentations for the Discovery Competition only a few days away, we were given all morning to work on our inventions. Jax hadn't joined in very much over the past week. He'd kept to himself, scribbling on bits of paper and staring into space. Because he still didn't know that we were now working on a completely different invention from the one he thought we were, we hadn't bothered trying to include him too much.

'We need your help in the storage cupboard,' Lottie said.

He looked up, surprised. 'I thought you two had everything covered.'

'Mostly,' I said. 'But we need you for this part.'

'OK.' He shrugged and followed us to the lost-property room.

As soon as we were inside, I closed the door behind us and turned the key in the lock.

'I'll look after it, Mo,' Lottie said, taking it and concealing it somewhere on her body. I couldn't see exactly where and I didn't want to think about it.

'What's going on, guys?' Jax said, looking confused. 'Mo? Is everything OK?'

'Everything isn't OK, Jax,' I said.

'And it's because of you,' said Lottie.

'What do you mean?' Jax said, pushing past us to the door. 'Let me out of here.'

'Not until you've answered our questions,' I said.

'Why are you doing this, Mo? What's your problem?'

'We know what you are,' Lottie said. 'And we know what you've done, so stop pretending you're Mo's friend.'

'I'll shout for help if you don't let me out,' Jax said – that dark look that I'd seen before clouding over his face.

'Shall I gag him?' Lottie said, turning to me.

'What? That's crazy!' I said.

'But we don't want him making too much noise.'

'How will he answer our questions if he's gagged?' I said.

'Good point,' she said.

'Anyway,' I said, 'we're not going to hurt him.'

'We aren't?' Lottie said.

I looked at Jax. 'No, we aren't. We're not like his mum and dad.'

'What do you know about my mum and dad?'
Jax said.

'We know plenty,' Lottie said. 'But what we
don't know is what they did to Mo's dad.'

Jax looked at the floor. 'I don't know what
you're talking about.'

'I don't believe you,' I said.

'That's because he's lying his pants off,' Lottie
said.

'Just tell us, Jax. I need to know what happened
to him. He's my *dad*.'

'Yeah, and I have to look out for my dad, too,'
Jax said. 'Only total jerks betray their own family.'

'But you aren't like them, Jax,' I said.

He turned away. I thought about punching
him. Part of me wanted to punch him. And I was
totally sure that Lottie wanted to punch him.
Probably in the nuts. But I knew that wouldn't get
me the answers I wanted; it would just make him
hate me.

'Please tell me,' I said. 'We're friends. You've
come to my house. My mum's cooked you dinner
and you've eaten with my family. You owe me
this.'

'I can't,' he said.

'Time to get heavy then,' Lottie said, cracking her knuckles and doing some lunges.

'What are you doing?' I said.

'Warming up, of course.'

'I told you, we're not hurting him.'

Lottie pulled me into a corner. 'Are we doing good cop/bad cop here?'

'No!' I said. 'I'm serious.'

'But he's not going to tell us anything.'

'Then we'll find another way.'

I turned back to Jax. 'Will you help us, Jax? Please.'

'No. Let me out of here now.'

'Let him out, Lottie,' I said.

'Are you sure? I've been practising this move where I squeeze his head between my knees, do this sort of twist, and throw him to the floor.'

'I'm sure,' I said.

'Boring,' she said, producing the key from somewhere and unlocking the door.

Jax ran out the door and out of school. We didn't see him again.

After that morning, we stopped seeing the Junkers everywhere we went. There was no sign of Mr

Gideon crawling up the streets behind us in his van. We didn't get any visits from Lorelai and, when we looked at the windows, there was no movement from the curtains to suggest anyone was looking out. Jax never came back to school.

'Well, that's a relief, at least,' Lottie said.

'Is it?' I wasn't so sure. It didn't feel like the end of the trouble – it felt like the start of something worse.

We'd decided not to risk another visit to the Junker house. Instead we focused all of our efforts on the Discovery Competition. We knew we had to win and, even though it was the last thing we felt like doing, we tried to put the distractions out of our minds and do the best job we could.

Discovery Day

Mo

When the morning of 31st October came around, we were ready to go.

'Have you attached the device?' Lottie said.

'Of course.'

'Have you turned it on?'

'Yes. I'm not an idiot.'

'Do you have everything else we need?'

'Just leave it to me, Lottie. I've got everything covered. I packed the bag and checked it three times last night and again this morning.'

It was an enormous day and we were both nervous and grumpy. Our first challenge was going to be getting to school safely. We didn't think it was likely that the Junkers would come for us until later in the day, because the solar flares weren't happening until the evening. But still, we were jumpy.

Our second challenge was going to be presenting our Discovery Competition invention. I was confident that our idea was solid, and Lottie had been working hard on what she called 'a compelling one-woman dramatic piece' to go with it. My main worry was whether or not the device would work when it came to the demonstration.

After all that, we would then have to get through the rest of the day without being taken by the Junkers. We had no Hector to look out for us, and no way of defending ourselves against an attack. Mr Gideon was one of the largest people I'd ever seen and, although she was small, I suspected that Lorelai could be vicious. And Jax... I had no idea what he would do. He was a mystery.

'Let's go, then,' Lottie said, buttoning up her coat all the way to the top and pulling her hood tight around her face.

'Do you think they won't recognise you just because you've done your coat up?' I asked.

'Maybe,' she said. 'There's no harm in trying. Anyway, I feel more protected this way.'

'Your coat is made of wool, not armour.'

'But the wool is very thick, Mo,' Lottie said. 'And it's turquoise.'

'What difference does that make?'

'Turquoise is the strongest and most attack-proof colour,' Lottie said. 'Everyone knows that.'

'I really don't think they do,' I said.

'Says the boy in a navy parka. Lol.'

I had no idea what she found funny, but I thought it was better not to ask.

We walked to school as quickly as we could. The streets were damp, the sky a threatening grey and the wind stung my nose. There was no sign of the Junkers.

'I wish we knew where Hector was,' I said, looking at the sad, empty crossing.

'We do know – he's in jail,' Lottie said. 'And I'm sure the number of road fatalities has decreased since they threw him in the slammer.'

'Lottie! He's our friend!'

'I know, Mo, but he's not here any more. I'm just being practical. Sometimes you just have to let things go.'

We made it through the gates to the safety of the playground – the rainbow benches looking out of place against the rest of the dull, dreary world.

Lottie

Since we'd looked through Emma's box and discovered that Mo's dad had probably been abducted and murdered by the Junkers, he hadn't been the same. He was sad, and tired, and his crazy, flappy hair looked even more of a fright than it usually did.

I felt bad for him, but also a bit annoyed. At least he knew now that his dad hadn't chosen to leave – he'd been dragged away against his will. If he hadn't been junked, he would probably still be with Emma and Mo, and they would be a perfect, happy family. Mo only thought about what he'd lost, rather than being glad that his dad had turned out not to be a total jerk. Also, if Mo's dad hadn't been junked, Mo's mum wouldn't have met my dad, and we wouldn't be a family.

As we waited to do our presentation in front of the whole school, I held back my nerves by doing some vocal exercises.

'What the fluff are those noises?' Mo said, not understanding anything as usual.

'I'm warming up, obviously.'

'It's a science and design competition. Not sports day.'

'With that attitude, Mo, it'll be a miracle if we win. It's a good thing I'm in charge of the showpiece.'

'Oh no, Lottie. What are you going to do?'

'I'm going to thrill. I'm going to take their breath away. I'm going to make sure we win.'

'I'm going to be hiding under the stage in embarrassment.'

Lottie jumps out of her chair and starts shaking out her arms and legs

Mo:
Sit down, Lottie – what are you doing?

Lottie:
I'm going to re-enact our presentation for everybody.

Mo:
They don't need to see that. I wish I could un-see it.

Lottie:
But I'll be able to describe it better if I act it out. I can only give my all, Mo. I won't settle for anything less.

Mo *sighs*:
Try not to knock anything over.

Lottie:
We stood in the shadows at the side of the stage, the sense of anticipation biting at our tongues…

Mo:
What?

Lottie:
…The crowd leaning forward on their seats – a sea of eager faces gazing at us with eyes full of awe…

Mo:
We were on right at the end, so everyone had already sat there for over an hour. They were leaning forward because they wanted to leave and their eyes were full of boredom.

Lottie:
And then it happened.

Mo:

And then Lottie happened. She dimmed the lights. She had what sounded like a movie soundtrack playing. She'd got hold of a dry ice machine from somewhere…

Lottie:

I created an electrical atmosphere, then leapt onto the stage, illuminated under a single blue spotlight. And I sparkled.

Mo:

She'd covered herself in sequins. That was why she'd done her coat right up on the way to school.

Lottie:

I whipped the audience into a frenzy with my ribbon-twirling display.

Mo:

I still don't understand what that had to do with our invention.

Lottie:
It was symbolic, Mo. Ribbons represent loss and despair, and the rainbow of hope streaking through the stormy sky. Everyone knows that.

Mo:
Right.

Lottie:
Then I pulled the crowd into a gentle lull, as the music calmed and I acted out a monologue to demonstrate the type of situation that our invention would help to prevent.

Mo:
She fell to the ground, sobbing about her dog going missing. She threw tissues into the audience.

Lottie:
It was a 4D immersive experience.

Mo:
Then she shielded her eyes as the hall lit up really brightly, and gasped…

Lottie:

'...What is that I see? What is that glimmer of hope on the horizon...?'

Mo:

She crawled towards the side of the stage where I was standing, trying not to die.

Lottie:

'Morris Appleby,' I said, 'in the name of all that is good in the universe, please save me from my trauma...'

Mo:

She grabbed my arm and pulled me onto the stage.

Lottie:

Unfortunately, he wasn't sparkly because he refused to wear the sequins I got for him.

Mo:

Then I told them the stuff that was actually relevant. I talked about the future of nanotechnology and my ideas for picotechnology, and then I introduced our invention...

Lottie:

He did it surprisingly well considering his lack of dramatic flair.

Mo:

…Which Lottie insisted on calling the Pip and Tracey…

Lottie:

…™! Don't forget that, Mo, it makes it official.

Mo:

All we had left was the demonstration. I held my breath as I opened the laptop…

Lottie:

'As you can see,' he said, 'the Tracey has successfully located the Pip that is attached to our sister, Sadie. Using this device, we can pinpoint her exact position. And according to Tracey, Sadie is currently at…'

Mo:

79 Morello Road.

Lottie:

As the audience applauded, Mo and I looked at each other in shock.

Mo:

We realised that the Junkers didn't need to come after us – they'd found a way of making us go to them.

Lottie:

They had Sadie and we would have to rescue her.

Mo:

I was so afraid that I forgot the last line of the presentation.

Lottie:

Luckily, I am a true professional and I covered Mo's mess up with an interpretive dance.

Mo:

As Lottie was doing a strange, rolling, double leg-kick thing, I saw Miss Woods from the office come in and whisper to Mr Chartwell.

Lottie:

We walked off the stage to deafening applause…

Mo:

AKA – a bit of polite clapping…

Lottie:

…And Mr Chartwell took us back to our classroom and told us that there had been an accident.

Mo:

Mum had fallen down the stairs and been taken to hospital in an ambulance.

Lottie:

And Dad was coming to collect us.

Mo:

We grabbed our things and waited in the Hub, not knowing if Mum was OK, or if Sadie was OK.

Lottie:

It was the worst ten minutes of our lives.

Mo:
So far.

Lottie
'I don't want you to panic,' Dad said as soon as we were in the car.

'What happened? Is Mum OK?' Mo was paler than I'd ever seen him, and obviously trying not to cry.

'Emma is hurt but she's going to be fine,' said Dad. 'She was showing Lorelai something in your bedroom and she tripped, somehow, and fell down the stairs.'

'What did she trip on?' I asked.

'She's not sure,' Dad answered, glancing at me in the mirror. 'She said she definitely felt something catch her foot, but there was nothing at the top of the stairs.'

'Emma's not usually clumsy,' I said, looking at Mo. I think we both knew what, or rather who, had tripped Emma.

'Just one of those unfortunate accidents, I guess,' Dad said. 'We were lucky that Lorelai was there – she called me and an ambulance and took Sadie over to her house.'

'Are we going to get her now?' I said, as the car turned into Morello Road.

'Well, we thought it would be best if Sadie stays put for the moment,' Dad said. 'I'm going to take some bits up to the hospital for Emma later, and you two are going to spend the evening at Lorelai's. Her nephew is coming over so she's turning her house into a haunted house for Halloween. Doesn't that sound great?'

Mo and I looked at each other.

'We'd rather get Sadie back and stay with you. We should all be together at a time like this,' I said.

'I have to go to the hospital, Lottie,' Dad frowned.

'We'll come with you,' Mo said. 'I want to see Mum.'

'I know you do, Mo, but children aren't allowed to visit in the evenings.'

'We'll wait in the car then,' I said. 'We don't like Lorelai, and we don't want to go there.'

'Listen, kids – I really don't want to argue with you. I need to focus on Emma right now and it would be great if you guys could help me out. It will just be for a couple of hours.'

'When's Mum coming home?' Mo said.

'Hopefully later tonight, Mo. It won't be long, I'm sure. And, in the meantime, you have something fun to do to take your mind off it all. Your mum said you two already have costumes.'

'We have,' I said, resigning myself to the fact that we were going to have to go and get Sadie back ourselves.

'We'll have a quick dinner, you can get ready and then go over to number 79 for a night of spooky fun.'

Mo looked like he was going to be sick.

'Yay,' I said.

We walked through our front door and trudged upstairs to prepare ourselves.

'We should stick to the original plan, right?' Mo said, as I opened my bedroom door.

'Absolutely. The original plan, but with theatrics.' I went into my room and started pulling things out of my drawers. I was quite excited that we were going to face the Junkers wearing costumes. It could only work in our favour.

The Season Finale

Lottie

At 6:30, I made my entrance downstairs in my incredible costume.

'Wow!' said Dad.

'I know,' I said.

'Er, Lottie?' Mo said, from underneath his Teenage Mutant Ninja Turtle mask. 'No offence, but what are you supposed to be exactly?'

'Wonder Woman of course.'

I was wearing skinny-fit blue tracksuit bottoms with silver stars glued to them, a red vest with a gold W on the front, a red hoody, and arm cuffs over the top made out of foil. My hair was double French plaited.

'I don't remember her looking like that.'

'I made a few adjustments,' I said, pulling on my red hi-tops. 'Wonder Woman is awesome, but if you were going into battle in October, would you really wear tiny shorts and high-heeled boots, with your hair loose?'

'Well I wouldn't,' said Mo.

'Exactly. Nobody would – it's impractical. Girls can be superheroes without being half naked.'

'Quite right, Lottie.' Dad smiled. 'Are you ready to go?'

'Did you take the you-know-what?' I whispered to Mo.

'Yes, it made me feel a bit funny though. Did you?'

'I did. And I have equipped us with more. They're in my pumpkin bucket, just in case.'

'Oh, look – that must be Lorelai's nephew.' Dad waved at a small person dressed as a ghost who was standing at the Junkers' front door. 'Lorelai has our spare key in case you need anything and Emma and I will be back soon. Have fun, you two!'

'It's OK, Sadie,' I whispered. 'We're coming.'

We walked down the steps and across the road to where a faint purple glow seeped out from the open front door at number 79. As we walked up the path, the ghost boy disappeared into the dark house, leaving us to follow. We squeezed each other's hands and entered.

'Trick or treat?' I called out, to break the creepy silence.

'Don't ask them that,' Mo said. 'What a dumb question!'

'What else would I ask?' I said. 'It's Halloween.'

'How about "Where's our sister?"' Mo said.

'Where's our sister?' I shouted, but there was no response apart from the door creaking shut behind us.

For a moment we were in total darkness – darkness so thick you could swallow it. And then the music started. 'Who's Afraid of the Big Bad Wolf?' – the original cartoon version, but slowed right down so the voices were distorted. It was scratchy and jumpy, and sounded like it was coming from one of those old record players that you never see in the real world, only in scary movies.

'Where did they get a record player?' I whispered.

'Ebay, I suppose,' Mo said. 'What a lot of bother when they could have just played it from their laptop.'

'But it sounds much more sinister like this,' I said. 'You've got to admire their vision.'

'So what happens next?' Mo said and, at that moment, a burnt orange light soaked through the gloom to illuminate some scrawly writing on the wall: 'To get your sister you must walk through the haunted house, but beware – the BIG BAD WOLF IS COMING TO GET YOU!'

'Well, it's nice that they left us instructions,' he said, taking a step forward. 'Always good to have a clear plan.'

'And look at all the decorations,' I said, pointing at the cobwebs and hanging skeletons. 'They've really gone to a lot of effort. I guess they really want to scare us.'

'Downstairs first?' Mo said, his voice sounding a little shaky.

I nodded, and we walked down the hall to the kitchen.

All the junk that had been there last time we visited was gone. There were no electrical or body parts lying around. There was no bin, no food, no rubbish. It had been completely emptied out.

The music sounded more distant from here – I guessed it was coming from upstairs where I knew we would inevitably end up going. But we had to be thorough, so we started opening cupboards and looking under work surfaces, in case Sadie was trapped there.

'We should look in here,' Mo said, putting his hand on the door of the freezer.

'There's always a body in the freezer,' I said.

'I know. But we have to look.' I held my breath as he pulled open the door and then screamed as something jumped out at us. I hit out, trying to get it away from me.

'It's OK, Lottie,' Mo said. 'It's just a chocolate gateau.' He put it back in the freezer and closed the door. Typical Mo, tidying up after himself, even in the face of death.

'Are you alright?' he said, looking at me through his turtle face.

'Brilliant,' I said. 'Best jump scare I've had in ages. What's next?'

We moved from the kitchen into the living room. Like the kitchen, the living room had been emptied of anything that would make it homely. The bare floorboards creaked as we walked across them and the air felt cold. It smelt of dust and burning, and those jelly sweets that old people like, which have really disgusting flavours like rose and elderflower. A noose hung from the light fitting, swinging in the draft from the window. There was no sign of Sadie.

'Anywhere else to look down here?' I asked, not overly wanting to go upstairs.

'The cupboard,' Mo said, leading me back into the hall.

'Oh,' I gulped. The cupboard didn't sound like a lot of fun either. But it had to be checked.

Mo swung open the door under the stairs and we both jolted back, expecting something to leap out at us. Nothing did. Unfortunately, all that we could see inside the cupboard was utter darkness.

'We'll have to feel around,' I said to Mo.

He nodded. 'Together?'

We both stretched our hands into the black void in front of us. My mouth was desert dry as I waited for something to bite me or snatch me. My fingers inched forwards through dust and cobwebs until they touched something cold and slimy.

'What is that?' Mo said.

'Entrails?'

'I really hope not.'

'Splattered brain?'

'Let's not get carried away. It feels familiar – I'm going to scoop some out and have a look.' Mo pulled his hand out of the cupboard and opened it. It was full of some green substance that looked like a cross between jelly and bogies.

'Alien Goo,' Mo said. 'You can buy it at the Pound Shop.' He wiped his hand on his leg.

'At least it goes with your costume,' I said. 'There's nothing here, so we go upstairs?'

There was a sound behind us, something large moving through the house. We grabbed each other in fright. 'Who's afraid of the big bad wolf, the big bad wolf, the big bad wolf...?' suddenly grew louder.

My heart was thumping so hard, I thought it might explode out of my chest. Then we really would see some entrails. 'I guess that was the wolf.'

Junked

Mo

The wolf moved again, with a thud and a creak, and a shadow fell over us.

'Run!' I said to Lottie, and we dashed towards the stairs. As we started to climb, something slammed towards us from above. We both screamed – and I mean really screamed. I was too scared even to be embarrassed about screaming. A tall figure lurched into us, knocking us back down to the bottom of the stairs.

'Which way do we go?' Lottie shouted. 'Up or down, Mo? Up or down?'

A purple light came on upstairs, lighting up the creature that swung in front of us. It had a pumpkin head with an evil face carved into it, raggedy clothes and sticks and straw for arms.

'It's a fluffing scarecrow on a rope!' I said. I wanted to run out of the house so very badly. I had never been more afraid in my life. Lottie looked terrified – she was turning towards the front door.

'Sadie,' I said. To remind myself as much as to remind her.

'Sadie.' She nodded.

We pushed past the scarecrow and ran up the stairs.

'My room,' I said, looking into the place I had once loved most in the world, but which I was now scared to walk into.

'Your ex-room,' Lottie said, squeezing my hand. 'You have a new room now, Mo. This is just a sad, empty room in a sad, empty house.'

As we stepped inside, the door slammed shut behind us, making us both jump. On the back of the door was another sign: LOCKED IN. And then the room fell into total darkness.

With no light to see by, Lottie and I huddled against a wall, waiting to see what would be thrown at us next.

'I suppose this is payback for us locking Jax in the storage cupboard with us,' I said. 'I wish we hadn't done that.'

'We had good reason, Mo. And we didn't do anything to hurt him or frighten him.'

'It still wasn't right,' I said. 'He was my friend. Or at least I thought he was.'

'I am your friend, Mo,' a quiet voice said from the corner, as the light from a torch shone in our eyes.

'Jax?' I said.

'No time to explain,' Jax replied, putting his ghost costume into my hands. 'You have to swap costumes with me.'

'Why?' Lottie asked. 'Why should we do anything you say?'

'I said there was no time to explain,' Jax snapped. 'You never make anything easy, do you, Lottie?'

'She doesn't,' I agreed, pulling my costume over my head.

'I'm going to help you, but we have to be quick,' Jax said. 'I've let Sadie out of the cat flap and given her your spare key. I also gave her something to look after, that you have to promise to guard with your lives.'

'I don't...' Lottie started.

'We will,' I said. 'Thank you for letting her go.'

'When I open the bedroom door, I want you to push me towards my dad. He's dressed as a wolf, FYI.'

'Figures,' I said.

'Don't say anything, just follow my lead. And when you get the opportunity – run, as fast as you can.'

I could tell Lottie still didn't trust him, but I knew – I absolutely knew – that I could. 'Just do it, Lottie,' I said. Then I gave Jax a quick hug. 'Thank you.'

'Let's go,' he said, turning off the torch and reaching for the door handle.

As the door opened, I could see the huge shape of a wolf standing right outside. I shoved Jax towards it, and it yanked him by the arm. He struggled and fought, and Lottie seemed to catch on to the plan which, as it happened, was right up her street.

'Let him go!' she screamed. 'Fight him, Mo. Fight that hideous beast!'

The wolf snarled and dragged Jax-disguised-as-Mo into what used to be my mum's bedroom. 'Time?' he growled at Lorelai who was standing ready, with something in her hand.

'6:42,' she said, prowling towards turtle Jax. She ripped off his glove and rolled up his sleeve.

'No!' Lottie cried. 'Leave him alone, you despicable animals!'

'Shut up, you irritating brat,' Lorelai said, giving Lottie a hard slap around the face. Lottie fell back and put her hand up to her cheek, which was noticeably red, even in the dimly lit room.

'Get the cuff on,' said Mr Gideon.

'Oh – cuff!' Lottie said, recovering quickly from the slap. 'That's the perfect name for it. A junking cuff. Of course.'

'I'm glad you like the name,' Lorelai said, 'You'll be seeing it again very soon.' She put the cuff on Jax's wrist and it sort of moulded itself around his arm. It wasn't the cuff I'd found a month or so before; it was less finished. There were no markings and it wasn't as perfectly sleek. It looked sort of patched together. 'This is going to hurt, dear,' she said. 'But it can't be helped. We thought we'd solved everything when we got rid of your father and his genius prosthetic inventions, but it seems an irritating gift for science runs in the family. Now we have to stop you, too.'

'And I'm just tagging along, am I?' said Lottie, looking rather cross.

'Don't worry, we'll be back for you. Just in case. Now...' Lorelai turned to Gideon, 'Shall I do the honours, my love?'

'You're wearing the wrong eyes, princess,' he growled.

'Oh, silly me!' Lorelai giggled, put her hand to her eye and pulled out her eyeball, leaving a gaping black hole in her head. She rummaged around in her box for another one, and squeezed it into the socket until it made a low popping noise. Then she lowered her eye to a square-shaped panel on the cuff. It immediately started beeping.

'I love this part!' Lorelai clapped, as she started counting down. 'Ten, nine...'

Then Jax pulled off his mask.

'What?' Lorelai gasped. 'What's happening? Get it off him, Gideon!'

They both pulled at the cuff, which continued to beep.

'You know you can't stop it now, Mother,' Jax said, looking small and sad.

'Get the tools, Gideon! Find the tools!'

Lorelai and Gideon started tearing through a pile of boxes in the corner.

'Will you be OK, Jax?' I shouted, feeling like we really shouldn't have let him sacrifice himself.

'They'll come for me soon. I'll be OK.' He smiled reassuringly, but I felt terrified for him.

'At the Junkyard?' Lottie called, over the beeping and the music and the crash of boxes.

'Yes,' Jax said, 'And Mo, if he's still there – I'll find him.'

'Who?' Lottie shouted, as a bright purple light started to seep out of the cuff and surround Jax in a square-shaped bubble.

'Your dad!' he shouted, and his last few words disappeared as he did, leaving only darkness.

The empty cuff resumed its original shape and thudded to the floor.

'No!' Lorelai screamed. 'What have you done to my boy?'

'I'll junk him, right now,' Mr Gideon said.

'We can't – there isn't another flare…' Lorelai sobbed.

'…For three months,' Lottie finished.

'And there isn't another double flare for eight months,' I said.

'I don't care,' Mr Gideon raged, grabbing me by the arm, 'I'm doing it.'

'That's not a good idea,' Lottie said.

'I'll decide what's a good idea,' said Mr Gideon, and he picked up the cuff.

'Fine, if you really want to die, right here,

right now, I suggest you go ahead,' Lottie smiled.

'Show them what's in your bucket, Lottie,' I said.

She shoved it towards them. 'Glitter Balls (™).'

'What?' Lorelai snatched the bucket.

'They're my own invention. Cake-biscuit hybrids filled with edible glitter. Designed to fill the person who eats them with metal.'

'We've both eaten lots today,' I said. 'So if you try to junk either of us, we'll all be…'

'Blown to hell,' Lottie high-fived me.

Lorelai threw the bucket to the ground and howled. Mr Gideon punched the wall. It looked pretty ridiculous seeing as he was still in his wolf costumer.

'We have no time. We have to get our boy,' Lorelai said.

'Get everything together,' he said. He leered over at us. 'We'll be back for you.'

Lottie and I turned and ran down the stairs, past the scarecrow, to the front door. I pulled down the handle, and we ran out into the street, expecting every moment for one of them to come after us. Sadie was waiting for us at the top of the steps with the front door open. We flew inside, flung ourselves on Sadie, and sat on the floor trying to catch our breath for a few minutes.

'Not the happiest Halloween ever,' Lottie said.

I closed my eyes and willed my heart and lungs to be calm. 'And we didn't even get any candy.'

Lottie's Secret

Mo

Mum and Spencer came home later that evening. We told them Lorelai had dropped us off when they were on their way back, and Mum was in too much pain to ask many questions. She was just bruised, though – she would get better. We lied about what a great time we'd had and why I'd swapped my costume and when she was too exhausted to stay up any longer, we gave her a hug and went upstairs to talk. Schrodinger was curled up on my bed, sleeping. Sadie sat next to him and then pulled the other junking cuff from down the back of her pants.

'Your dad might be alive, Mo,' Lottie said. 'You might even get to see him one day. Aren't you happy?'

'I don't know,' I said. 'The whole thing is awful – it's hard to be happy about what is only a teeny tiny chance.'

'You're looking at it all wrong,' Lottie said.

'How's that?' I said. I felt quite cross with her –

she couldn't possibly understand what I'd been through.

'Mo, your dad was drugged by an evil ice cream man and transported, fighting every step of the way, I expect, to a hellish junkyard in an apocalyptic future. He didn't want to leave your mum and I'm certain he wouldn't have wanted to leave you.' Lottie looked at the floor. 'But my mum... Let me show you.' She ran out of the room and came back a minute later with a box.

'What's this?' I said.

'My secret box,' she said.

'Yes, I know that, but why are you showing me it?'

'I'm showing you what happened to my mum,' she said, pulling it open.

'I thought your mum was digging up dinosaurs, or inventing a cure for tonsillitis or something,' I said.

'My mum is in Luton.' Lottie tipped the contents of her box onto my bedroom floor. 'She lives with her new husband, Dirk, and their baby girl, Annabel. These are all the cards and letters she's sent me since she left.'

There were loads of them, all in different

coloured envelopes, with the same curly writing on the front. None of them were opened.

'Why haven't you read them?' I said.

'I don't know, really,' Lottie shrugged. 'I wanted to think she'd be coming back. I didn't want to hear about her enjoying her life with her new family.'

'But you have a new family, too,' I said, putting my arm around her.

'That's true.' She sniffed. 'And they're kind of great.'

'I never thought I wanted a sister, but I'm glad I have you and Sadie. And, if you like, you can share my mum. She really is the best.'

'She is. She smells like strawberries and pancakes,' Lottie said. 'Thanks, Mo.'

Lottie

The next day we stood at our open front door, looking over at number 79. The Junker house was dark, the curtains open, the rooms empty. They had gone. We walked to school feeling happier than we had for weeks.

'What's going on?' Mo asked, as we approached the main road to the sound of honking horns and angry shouts.

'Hector!' we said simultaneously, running to the crossing.

'We don't want you here!' A mum was shouting in Hector's face. 'We all saw you being taken away by the police.'

'No charges were brought,' Hector said.

'No smoke without fire, they say,' she yelled, waving her arms around.

'Madam, your face is terrifying, especially up close, and you're spitting on me rather a lot. Please back off.'

'How dare you?' she said, swinging her arm at him and knocking his hat off.

'Look at his hair,' I said, nudging Mo hard with my elbow. 'LOOK AT HIS HAIR!'

His hair was bright ginger and it stuck up in all different directions.

'He has your hair,' I said, gazing at him with her mouth open.

'There was no need for that,' Hector said to the mum. 'But as it happens, today is my last day, so you won't be seeing me again.'

'Thank god for that,' she said over her shoulder, and she walked over to the school, dragging her daughter behind her.

Hector picked his hat up and shoved it on his head, then turned and spotted us in the crowd. He smiled.

'I'll walk you home after school,' he said. 'We can have a good chat.'

We spent the day speculating about Hector. Or at least I did, while Mo fretted about the results of the Discovery Competition, which were going to be announced later that day. I wasn't worried at all – I knew we'd win. Our winners' certificate can be found in the evidence box – Exhibit P. We were super-proud.

After school, we waited for Hector to finish at the crossing, and then he walked with us towards home.

'Very happy to see you're both still here and in one piece,' he said. 'Or two pieces, rather. Not two pieces per person. A piece each? I'm glad you're OK.'

'And we won the competition,' Mo said, waving the certificate at him. He hadn't put it down since we'd been presented it in a special assembly. 'Now we have to improve the design and make another, better, prototype for the next stage.'

'You'll do a fantastic job, I'm sure,' Hector said.

'We were worried about you,' Mo said.

'I'm fine. Man of steel. They only choose the toughest people to be school crossing guards, you know.'

I couldn't hold back the questions any longer. 'What's your real name?'

'Hector.'

'We know that,' I said. 'I mean your real last name?'

'I can't tell you without breaking a lot of rules.'

'Tell us!'

'But the ripples!'

'Now that we've seen your hair, we've guessed anyway – you might as well just say so.'

'I don't think you've guessed correctly,' he said.

'If you'd found the clues in my notes, you wouldn't be asking me these questions.'

'What clues in your notes?' Mo said. 'There were clues in your notes?'

'I thought it would be fun,' Hector said. 'And, also, it was a way of telling you without breaking the rules and telling you. Technically speaking.'

'You're Mo's grandad,' I blurted.

'That's so stupid, Lottie,' Mo said. My granddads both have brown hair. I know them. One lives in Ireland and the other one in Clacton. He is definitely not my grandad.'

Hector was laughing really hard. 'Ha! Yes, I am definitely NOT Mo's grandad.'

'Who are you then?' I said. 'You must be related to Mo – that kind of hair should only really come around once in a lifetime. And once would have been too often, IMHO.'

'What?' Hector said.

'In my honest opinion, obviously. Everybody knows that.'

'I thought it was humble opinion?' said Mo.

'There is nothing humble about my opinion, Mo,' I said.

'That's true.'

'Seeing as you've half guessed,' Hector interrupted, 'maybe I could tell… but, if I do, you absolutely cannot tell the authorities in the future that I did, or they won't let me come back again. And you might need me.'

'JUST TELL US!' I yelled.

'My name is Hector Appleby…'

'You are related to Mo! I knew it!'

'Actually, my last name is Appleby-Button. I'm related to both of you. I'm Mo's brother, and I'm your brother. Your baby brother! Surprise!'

Lottie is interrupted by Mo's very loud laughter

Lottie:
Shut up, Mo.

Mo:
But it was the funniest thing! Lottie was so shocked – you should have seen her face.

Lottie:
Well, neither of us were expecting that answer, were we? It was absurd.

Mo *still laughs*:
It was awesome.

Lottie:
We looked back at Hector's notes and found the clues.

Mo:
They were really obvious when we knew to look for them.

Lottie:
I bet nobody else spotted them either. What kind of nut job hides clues in bits of writing?

Mo:
Er, Lottie – we've just hidden…

Lottie:
Anyway – just a few more ends to tie up here before we go. I'm starving and I think we're getting Domino's for dinner.

Mo:
Ooh, Domino's. Let's hurry.

Lottie:

You're probably wondering what Jax's last words were – the ones he shouted to us through the giant tesseract before he died.

Mo:

He didn't die, Lottie, he time-jumped to the Junkyard.

Lottie:

Same thing.

Mo:

Not the same thing at all.

Lottie:

Anyway, what he told us was a clue – a clue to the location of the Junkyard.

Mo *gives Lottie a harsh side-eye*:

We've hidden it amongst the evidence in this box. Have a look – see if you can work it out. And if you find it, keep it safe.

Lottie:

So, we have the cuff and the clue…

Mo:

…And we're going to use them to try to work out where the Junkyard is so we can find my dad. We know the Junkers will come back for us…

Lottie:

…But thanks to Sadie, we have a list of the solar flares, so we also know we have some time.

Mo:

This vlog and these documents might be the only record of everything that happened.

Lottie:

So, if we disappear…

Mo:

You hold the key to finding us.

Lottie:

If the Junkers know you have it, they'll probably come after you, too. So stay alert and trust no one.

Mo:

Don't say that, Lottie. We never would have made it this far if we hadn't trusted each other.

Lottie:

OK, not no one. But read through the info about how to spot a Junker again. Memorise the poem: Jumbled face and body parts, they're masters of disguise; Unhealthy sugar cravings for biscuits cakes and pies…

Mo:

Never be alone with them; Kandy is their bait.

Lottie:

Equip yourself and RUN or The Junkyard is your fate.

Mo:

Repeat it to yourself until you know it back to front…

Lottie:

…And keep it in your head at all times.

Mo:

Because if you forget…

Lottie:

Or get yourself caught…

Mo:

We'll be seeing you at The Junkyard.

The tense silence is broken by the arrival of a young girl, who flings the door open and bowls into the room like she's leading a parade.

Mo *huffing*:

We weren't finished, Sadie. Now we're going to have to do that bit all over again.

Sadie:

Perowt mewl prew.

Mo:

Maybe you do have the right to be here, but it's not about that. It's about getting across the seriousness of the situation to the people watching.

Sadie:
Mrow.

Mo:
It's my room and I get to choose who comes in.

Lottie:
Mo!

Mo:
Can I not have any privacy anymore?

Sadie:
Hiss.

Lottie *jumping up and down and tugging Mo's arm*:
Mo!

Mo *his face getting redder by the second*:
Argh! What is it, Lottie?

Lottie:
You did it! You understood Sadie!

Mo:

Oh my god. I did. I understood her.

There is a moment of silence. The three children stare at each other and a smile creeps across Mo's face.

Lottie:

We have to celebrate! Who wants ice cream?

Mo:

You're kidding, right?

Mo, Lottie and Sadie leave the bedroom and the sound of their footsteps can be heard clattering down the stairs. A moment later, one set of footsteps returns, and Mo's face appears as he leans over the camera. He smiles and reaches for the off button.

END OF RECORDING

Acknowledgements

First of all, I'd like to thank the people who have worked so hard on this book. I'm incredibly lucky to be supported by the wonderful team at Firefly – Rebecca Lloyd, who did an amazing job of editing *Mo and Lottie*, Penny Thomas, Meg Farr and Janet Thomas. Everyone at Firefly is brilliant, committed and exceptionally lovely. Thanks to you all.

An enormous thank you goes to Gareth Conway, who created the most fantastic illustrations for the book. I just love them, and feel very lucky to have you on the *Mo and Lottie* team. Thanks, also, to Kathryn Davies for the awesome cover design.

My agent, Kirsty McLachlan, deserves a medal for putting up with my moments of panic and frustration! Thank you for always being supportive and brilliant, and for guiding me with such patience.

Thanks, as always, to the Golden Egg Academy. I wouldn't be an author if it wasn't for Imogen Cooper; and the continuing support of the Eggs never fails to surprise me in the nicest way. There are so many of you that I can't name everyone, but please know you all have my heartfelt thanks.

I wouldn't survive this whirlwind of a journey without my wonderful author friends, especially Eloise Williams, Vanessa Harbour and BB Taylor. Huge thanks go to Vashti Hardy for the wonderful cover quote and for championing *Mo and Lottie* from the start. And to my dear friend, Lorraine Gregory: you are such an important part of my life, and I couldn't manage without you.

There are people whose support of my books has made a massive difference, and I am so grateful. Jo Clarke, Ashley Booth, Scott Evans, Jo Cummins, Fiona Sharp and all my friends at Waterstones Uxbridge (especially Jane Carter): I owe you all a drink.

The past year has seen me travel the country, visiting schools and meeting thousands of readers. My family have adjusted with good grace and enthusiasm, and given me such loving support, so, thanks and love to Dean, Mia, Stanley, Helena, Luis and Teddy. Thanks, also, to Dean for helping me with all the science stuff!

Being invited into a school is a privilege, and I am grateful to the teachers and children who have welcomed me. Some of my days spent at schools have been truly life-changing, and have meant more to me than I can express. So thank you to every other school I've visited, especially St Michael's, Little Plumstead, Lansdowne, Holy Cross, St Mary's, St Silas, Springwood Heath, Christ Church, Blyton and Colham Manor.

I'm really lucky to have a network of friends and family rooting for me: Mum, Dad, Julie, David, Alfie, Nic, Laura, Emma, Sarah, Jay, and all my aunties, uncles and cousins – thank you so much!

This book is full of hidden messages, many of them contributed by readers and supporters. Thank you so much to everyone who offered a name, or a date. I LOVE that this book has a little piece of all of you inside it.

Also by Jennifer Killick

Alex Sparrow and the Really Big Stink

Selected for the Summer Reading Challenge 2017
Longlisted for the Shrewsbury Big Book Award 2018

Alex Sparrow is a super-agent in training. He is also a human lie-detector. Working with Jess, who can communicate with animals, they must find out why their friends – and enemies – are all changing into polite and well-behaved pupils. And exactly who is behind it all.

Alex Sparrow and the Really Big Stink is a funny, mid-grade novel full of farts, jokes and superhero references. Oh, and a rather clever goldfish called Bob. In a world where kids' flaws and peculiarities are being erased out of existence, Alex and Jess must rely on what makes them different to save the day.

£6.99

'A brilliantly bonkers, side-splitting, superhero story.' **M.G. Leonard**

Alex Sparrow and the Furry Fury

Selected for the Summer Reading Challenge 2018
#PrimarySchoolBookClub pick June 2018

Catching the school's runaway guinea pigs is not really giving Alex job satisfaction, but how can he find a bigger test for his and Jess's awkward superpowers? Jess is more worried about the bullied new boy, whose Mum runs the local animal sanctuary. To befriend him she gets a voluntary job there, but she soon realises that something is very wrong; the animals are terrified. People start reporting strange events: things missing, property destroyed, and the local squirrels have turned mean. The police have no suspects. It looks more and more like a job for Agent Alex…

£6.99

'What a page turner! The terrible twists in this book will keep children guessing until the end… An innocent, funny and exciting read, with characters you wish you could be friends with.' **BookTrust**

'*Furry Fury* is the second book in this terrific and genuinely hilarious series … a worthy selection for the 2018 Summer Reading Challenge.' **Previewer's Pick by Caroline Sanderson, The Bookseller**

'Cracking adventure full of daft stunts, villainous villains and one far-too-cute hedgehog.' **James Nicol**